"If you were enchanted by Woody Allen's *Midnight in Paris,* you will love immersing yourself in another historical period filled with wit and panache, *Nick & Jake.* The Richards brothers bring their playful creativity and intelligent writing to this treasure of a book."

—Valerie Plame Wilson, former CIA operations officer

"Carraway and Barnes begin as proxies for their creators; their letters recall familiar cadences in Fitzgerald's and Hemingway's prose. It's a great hook, but as the novel spools out and hijinks ensue—political, romantic, sexual—Nick and Jake acquire more distinction. Bidding them good-bye a second time is sweet sorrow indeed. In addition to providing incisive political commentary, resurrecting cultural icons, and breathing life into fictional heroes, the Richards brothers shine a warm, nostalgic light on the lost art of letter writing. *Nick & Jake* approximates the ebb and flow of missives between friends, lovers, even adversaries. Offered here are the rhythms of relationships fostered through the shared mind-space of language, and the sweet anticipation of awaiting a response. *Nick & Jake* proves the epistolary art may yet live."

—Robert Burke Warren, Chronogram.com

NICK
&
JAKE

NICK
&
JAKE

An
Epistolary
Novel

Jonathan Richards
and Tad Richards

ARCADE PUBLISHING • NEW YORK

To Claudia Jessup and Pat Richards.
We couldn't have done this—or anything else,
come to think of it—without you.

Arcade Publishing books may be purchased in bulk at special discounts for
sales promotion, corporate gifts, fund-raising, or educational purposes. Special
editions can also be created to specifications. For details, contact the Special Sales
Department, Arcade Publishing, 307 West 36th Street, 11th Floor, New York,
NY 10018 or info@skyhorsepublishing.com.

Arcade Publishing® is a registered trademark of Skyhorse Publishing, Inc.®, a
Delaware corporation.

Visit our website at www.arcadepub.com.

10 9 8 7 6 5 4 3 2 1

Library of Congress Cataloging-in-Publication Data is available on file.

ISBN: 978-1-62872-320-5

Printed in the United States of America

1953

I t was a year unlike any other. On January 20, Gen. Dwight Eisenhower was sworn in as President of the United States in a ceremony broadcast to 21 million black-and-white television sets. The hunt for Reds was in full swing, spearheaded by Joe McCarthy in the U.S. Senate. On Broadway, Arthur Miller attacked the communist witch hunts with *The Crucible*; and in the movies, Elia Kazan was making *On the Waterfront* in defense of naming names. Television newsman Edward R. Murrow began work on an exposé of the tactics of Senator McCarthy.

In June, convicted atomic spies Julius and Ethel Rosenberg died in the electric chair, leaving two orphaned boys. (A half-century later, Soviet documents confirmed Ethel's innocence.) The prosecution had been spearheaded by an ambitious young lawyer named Roy Cohn, who was now Chief Counsel for Senator McCarthy's committee. Cohn and his friend G. David Schine left on a book-banning junket through American government libraries in Europe, to the embarrassment of the American diplomatic corps, and the great entertainment of the European press. When Schine was drafted later that year, Cohn's threats to retaliate by exposing the Army as riddled with Reds eventually led to McCarthy's condemnation by the Senate.

Around the world there was turmoil. America was bogged down in an undeclared war in Korea. In Vietnam, France (with quiet American help) struggled to hold onto the vestiges of its Indochina empire, while back in Paris, governments spun in and out of power through a revolving door. Soviet dictator Joseph Stalin died. America announced it had the H-bomb; a few months later, so did the USSR, and the dance of terror between the two superpowers was joined.

Two of Eisenhower's chief advisers made anti-Communism their personal crusade. John Foster Dulles was named Secretary of State, while across town, his brother Allen was sworn in as the first civilian director of the fledgling Central Intelligence Agency. While Foster articulated the Domino Theory, Allen's CIA would undertake spying on Americans, mind-control experiments, assassinations, and coups. Among its accomplishments was the subsidizing of cultural organizations, including the creation of the international leftist journal *Encounter*, edited by a former City College Trotskyite named Irving Kristol (later a founder of neoconservatism) and British poet Stephen Spender. More significant, the CIA instituted a policy of nation-building, orchestrating the overthrow of the democratically elected governments of reformers Jacobo Arbenz in Guatemala and Mohammed Mossadegh in Iran. Guatemalans got a repressive military junta, and Iranians saw the restoration of the U.S.-friendly Shah to the Peacock Throne.

It was a year for scientific miracles. Dr. Jonas Salk created a vaccine against polio. Drs. Francis Crick and James Watson described the structure of DNA as a double helix, and in Denmark, Dr. Christian Hamburger performed the world's first sex change operation on a young American G.I. named George Jorgensen.

This collection of letters from that eventful year casts a wide net over characters and events both fact and fiction. At the center of the action are a couple of characters who made their way from the Twenties and meet here for the first time: Nicholas Carraway, Republican functionary and one-time novelist, and Jacob Barnes, expatriate newsman. These gentlemen were previously thought to be the creations of a couple of novelists named F. Scott Fitzgerald and Ernest Hemingway, but it is revealed here for the first time that Nick and Jake are real historical figures. Fitzgerald and Hemingway never existed. That's our story, and we're sticking to it.

History has been tweaked and bent to suit our purposes, but a decent respect to the opinions of mankind has kept us close to the line of essential historical truths. Some of the most beloved works of 20th-century American literature have been cheerfully pillaged. Names have not been changed, and the innocent will have to shift for themselves.

NAMING NAMES

CHARACTER LEGEND
(in order of appearance)

Nick Carraway (The Great Gatsby): In his youth he wrote a novel; now he's a patriotic American who wants only to serve his country ... if his country still has a place for him.

Jake Barnes (The Sun Also Rises): Expatriate, legendary journalist, he's covered Europe for three decades. Once he thought of writing a novel, but never got beyond telling his story late at night to a sympathetic bartender.

George/Christine Jorgensen (sex-change pioneer): She's looked at life from both sides now, and she knows secrets of the heart ... and secrets that can spell trouble.

Allen Dulles (CIA director): As the first director of the fledgling CIA, he has ambitions to control the world ... if he can control his own associates.

Ronnie Gilchrist (Nick & Jake): You can take the girl out of Winnetka ... and with the right influences, you can take Winnetka out of the girl.

Irving Kristol (co-founder, Encounter; neo-conservative pioneer): Could the liberal editor of a leftist intellectual journal have a secret agenda?

Senator Joseph McCarthy (junior senator from Wisconsin): He had the Commies crying Uncle Sam ... until he took a shine to the army.

John Foster Dulles (Secretary of State): Ike's right hand, the Dulles who played by the book.

Margery Pyle Carraway (Nick & Jake): Nick's estranged wife--it was the little things that drove them apart.

Dorothy Kilgallen (newspaper columnist, radio/ TV personality): Scandal was her line, the Little Red Thrush her mystery guest.

Alden Pyle Carraway (The Quiet American): Nick's son; expatriate, rebel, idealist; he did great harm out of good intentions.

Larry Darrell (The Razor's Edge): For him, the line between enlightenment and espionage was as thin as a razor's edge.

Irving Sheinbloom (A Mighty Wind): Folk music was his business, but a pretty girl could send him on top of Old Smokey.

Jackie Susann (author, Valley of the Dolls): From her room in the Martha Washington Hotel for Women, she had her own brand of New York savvy for Ronnie Gilchrist.

Little Johnny Phillips (founder, The Mamas and the Papas): Musically ahead of his time, come Monday morning he was still a kid.

Lee Hays and Ronnie Gilbert (The Weavers): Members of the popular folk quartet, they needed a replacement for Pete Seeger, but Ronnie Gilchrist was not to be their darling.

The other guy in the Weavers: Whose name no one could ever remember.

Roy M. Cohn (Senator McCarthy's top aide): He found Commie filth on every bookshelf, and a Red in every closet.

Davey Schine (McCarthy investigator): Did his heart belong to "Daddy," or did every little breeze seem to whisper Maurice?

Thomas Fowler (The Quiet American): British journalist. Saigon was his beat, Americans were his *bête*--especially the quiet ones.

Stephen Spender (British poet): A close Encounter with the CIA was more than he bargained for.

Robert Cohn (The Sun Also Rises): Roy's uncle, CIA maverick. He thought the sun also rose for him ... but only if he could make it set over Jake Barnes.

Maurice Chevalier (entertainer, collaborator): He sang for the Germans, but he didn't remember it well.

Clare Boothe Luce (author, ambassador): She could make Time stand still, but for Nick she was arsenic and old Luce.

Simone de Beauvoir and Jean-Paul Sartre (existentialists): These French intellectuals were more than willing to make Nick Carraway the toast of Paris.

Kim Philby (British/Soviet double agent): Could he be trusted with the deepest secrets of American intelligence?

Clyde Tolson (associate director, FBI): Special friend of the FBI Director, he knew all the secrets ... and he knew Christine.

Mary Richards (<u>The Mary Tyler Moore Show</u>): With Ronnie as her mentor, she would make it after all.

Bud Powell (American jazz pianist): A tormented genius who would do anything for a friend.

Francis Paudras (French jazz critic): Journalist, jazz lover, he would work till 'round midnight to help Jake.

Helen Fowler (<u>The Quiet American</u>): Thomas Fowler's estranged wife ... but no divorce.

Dr. Christian Hamburger (Danish surgeon): The Stein Ericksen of sex-change surgery.

Stein Ericksen (Olympic champion): The Christian Hamburger of Alpine skiing.

Jerry Wexler (record producer): Co-founder of Atlantic Records with **Ahmet Ertegun**, he had an ear for talent, and Ronnie Gilchrist was talent.

Ray Charles, Ruth Brown, LaVern Baker, Chuck Berry, David "Fathead" Newman (recording artists): They each had something to teach Ronnie about music ... and life.

Lady Brett Ashley (<u>The Sun Also Rises</u>): An old girlfriend of Jake's, she's chosen the path of enlightenment, but she hasn't lost her sense of entitlement.

Bill Buckley (author, conservative icon): A schoolyard bully.

Sloan Wilson (author, <u>The Man in the Gray Flannel Suit</u>): An American in Paris who picks up a novel idea from Nick.

James Baldwin (author): As an expatriate in another country, he was saving his fire for next time.

Lamont Cranston (The Shadow): A wealthy young man about town who uses his power to cloud men's minds to influence the course of history.

William Fromme (father of Manson Family member): Margery's husband-to-be, raising his daughter Lynette to be a squeaky-clean American patriot.

Dr. Mohammed Mossadegh (prime minister of Iran 1951-1953): He believed American-style democracy could change the Middle East.

Art Buchwald (journalist): A young protégé of Jake's at the Paris Tribune.

Shah Mohammed Reza Pahlevi (Shah of Iran): A young protégé of Allen Dulles's on the Peacock Throne.

Jimmie Dodd (host, The Mickey Mouse Club): A TV director with some Mickey Mouse ideas about what makes a show work.

Albert Camus (author, philosopher): Another French intellectual absurdly eager to champion Nick.

Howard Koch (screen writer): An American writer and exile of conscience from McCarthyism. Here's looking at you, kid.

Sen. Prescott Bush (senator, war profiteer): The Presidency--maybe not today, maybe not tomorrow, but soon and for the rest of your life.

George H. W. Bush (CIA desk officer): Can Dulles trust him?

Jean Renoir (movie director) and Yves Montand (movie star): They hope to make a movie version of Nick's gangster novel.

Francoise Sagan (author, Bonjour Tristesse): She flashes a certain smile at Nick, but he's not so certain.

Maurice Girodias (publisher, Venus in Bondage, The Story of O, Lolita, Lady Chatterley's Lover): He has no trouble in promising Nick an Olympian advance.

Gen. Raoul Salan (founder, Terrorist Group Against Algerian Independence): In case we need a Falangist takeover of France.

Edward R. Murrow (legendary pioneer of television journalism): He wants his old pal Jake to join him in a brave new enterprise in electronic journalism. Good night, and good luck.

Blossom Dearie (American jazz singer): American expatriate who takes Ronnie under her wing.

York Harding (The Quiet American): A writer of books, he helped Alden understand the role of the West.

THE LETTERS

Nicholas Carraway
Assistant Undersecretary of State for
European Affairs
Department of State
Washington, D.C.

Mr. Jacob Barnes
Paris Herald Tribune
38, rue de Berri
Paris 16e, France

January 26, 1953

Dear Mr. Barnes,

We have not met, but I'm a great admirer of
yours. I am an avid reader of your byline
in the Trib, and one of the treasured books
in my library is your memoir of Paris in
the Twenties, A Lost Generation. It's clear
to me that you have a greater understanding
than most Americans of Europe, and of France
in particular.

From your vantage point you will see the
urgent need, in a world still recovering
from the wounds of war, of spreading abroad
the good news of American ideals, American
values, and American progress. We showed
the world our might in the armed conflict;
now, with the architect of that victory
leading from the White House, we must
seize the opportunity to show the world

our compassion, our moral compass, our democratic ideals, and the beacon of hope that shines from Lady Liberty's torch.
I am hoping that you can assist me in gathering some information that may prove helpful to your country. There is, as you know, a bit of hysteria in Washington these days over the influence of International Communism in U.S. libraries abroad. You and I are men of the world. We know how damaging this sort of heavy-handed Puritan zeal can be to American prestige abroad when it gets out of hand.

I wonder if you can help me by compiling an informal list of books in embassy libraries that might be considered objectionable, so we can make a few timely removals and defuse the situation before it gets embarrassing. I realize this is an imposition, but I hope you will see the merit in this kind of preemptive strike.

Very Truly Yours,

Nicholas Carraway
Assistant Undersecretary of State for European Affairs

Jacob Barnes
Paris Herald Tribune
38, rue de Berri
Paris 16, France

Nicholas Carraway
Ass't Undersec. of State for European
Affairs
Department of State
Washington, D.C.

January 29, 1953

Dear Mr. Carraway,
I would sooner swim the Marne.

Yours Truly,

Jake Barnes

Jake Barnes
1 rue de Fleurus
Paris 6, France

Mr. George Jorgensen
Royal Hospital
Copenhagen, Denmark

Jan. 29

George--

Good luck with the operation.

Me? It's a damned interesting suggestion,
but no thanks! I am sitting here in the
Closerie des Lilas watching some Bryn Mawr
girls get drunk on white wine and what
unscrupulous restaurateurs assure them is
absinthe, imagining themselves in the fairy
tales their fairy college professors told
them. I too am doing my damnedest to get a
drunk on, thanks to your proposal. It gives
me the willies to think about it. Please. I
already gave at the office.

Not that I haven't been tempted to make some changes in my life. When Brett went to Nepal last year, I kept thinking I was the one who should become a goddamn Buddhist monk and disappear from the world. I sometimes wish I'd written the novel about her I wanted to write, instead of pissing it away on A Lost Generation. You know, I told the whole story of her and me and Cohn and that damned bullfighter to a bartender one night around two in the morning. The sonofabitch pretended to be interested, but he was probably really hoping I'd shut the hell up so he could close up and go back to a clean, well-lighted room. It must have sounded like a bunch of nada to him, but it was fine and true and the next day it was gone and I had nothing to show for it but the hangover. And then I walked into the Crillon Bar that night and met you. And I thought, now there is one hell of a novel just begging to be written. Watch out for writers, Georgie my girl. We'll eat you alive and suck the marrow from your bones. That at least is our intention. Sometimes I even disgust myself, but writing is a goddamn disease.

Anyway, Brett was all right. And you're all right, George. You're a swell guy, and I guess this may be the last time I'll be able to say that.

And me? Fuck it, I guess I'll wait for the day they can sew the goddamn thing back on. What about yours? You won't be using it.

Yours always,

Jake

Nicholas Carraway
Assistant Undersecretary of State for
European Affairs
Department of State
Washington, D.C.

Mr. Allen Dulles
Director, Central Intelligence Agency

Jan. 30, 1953

Dear Mr. Dulles,

I wrote Barnes as per our discussion.
Enclosed please find a copy of his response.
He's a bit talkier than General McAuliffe at
Bastogne, but not by much.

This may be the wrong way to get to someone
like Barnes. If the idea is to use important
journalists to shape opinion in France,
Barnes is our man. But we're not going
to get to him just by waving the flag. I
don't know much about Europe, but I read
Barnes' book, <u>A Lost Generation</u>, and I guess
all of us followed the reporting he and
Murrow did during the war. This is a tough,
independent-minded guy.

I'm not sure I'm the best man for this job.
Do you have any contacts who are closer
to Barnes? I know he's on the board of

<u>Encounter</u>, which is a leftish intellectual
magazine edited by a guy named Irving
Kristol. Maybe Kristol could help us?
Or I'll be glad to take another stab at him,
but next time let me use my own approach.

Very Truly Yours,

Nicholas Carraway
Assistant Undersecretary of State

By special courier
Feb 2, 1953

Carraway--

We don't have any connection with Kristol or anyone else at <u>Encounter</u>. So you're our man. Europe is crucial to our goals. Barnes is the key to setting that up. He's the most authoritative voice in our European press corps. People listen to what he has to say, and I'm counting on you to make sure he says the right things. I've got the feeling Barnes may know things he shouldn't, but we don't know what or how much. Is his head on straight? Can he cause problems? Does he have beans to spill? And is he likely to spill them?

Sure, try Barnes your way. You're the ad man--sell him. And didn't you write a book once, too? Give him the old literary brotherhood.

Make it work, Nick. We need to start shaping opinion now.

Dulles

Nicholas Carraway
Assistant Undersecretary of State for
European Affairs
Department of State
Washington, D.C.

February 2, 1953

Dear Mr. Barnes,

The Marne can be pretty damn chilly this
time of year. Let's see if we can't find
another way.

I think I made a bad start, and I apologize
for that. I'd like to excuse my clumsy
approach by pleading new-boy jitters. I've
just come on board here at State, and am
trying to find out how I fit in. The first
months of a new administration are more
chaotic than I'd imagined, and we're all
feeling our way along. I don't even know
where the men's room is yet.

As I mentioned in my first letter, I'm
a great admirer of your writing. <u>A Lost
Generation</u> felt like what Paris in the
Twenties must have been. It's a hell of a
book, the real thing. And your dispatches
from Europe, during the War and since,
are better than anyone alive is doing.
It's all given me the illusion of knowing

a bit about you, and of course you know
nothing at all about me. So I'll give you
an autobiographical sketch by way of an
introduction, if you'll indulge me. I'm a
bit of a writer myself.

When I was a young man I lived for a season
on the Eastern seaboard, among people who
were privileged and careless and very rich.
I grew up in the Midwest, and the Northeast
had an irresistible lure to a boy lying on
his bed looking out over twilit cornfields
and cattle pastures, and dreaming of the
center of the universe.

I came East in the fall of '16 to do my
university work at New Haven, and from there
only a few miles of railroad track separated
me from my dreams of a fortune in the New
York City bond market.

As it happened, I took the long way around.
The Great War intervened, and with a minimum
of reflection and an excess of romantic
impulsiveness, I joined the Norton-Harjes
ambulance service under the French--my carte
d'identité shows a slim, tousle-haired boy
with a dimpled jaw, a pendulous lower lip,
and eyes as yet unacquainted with tragedy.
Then, when America got into the War, I
signed up for a crash course in the Serbo-
Croatian language, and found myself assigned
to General Pershing's staff as a translator/
interrogator. I was close enough to the

action to hear and smell it, but I never really had the chance to test myself under fire--or in the chilly waters of the Marne, though Lord knows I got to see them, eddying mud and blood. That memory will last me a good deal longer than my Serbo-Croatian. Things learned fast are forgotten fast. We never captured any Serbo-Croatians for me to interrogate, and I hardly remember a word of it. "Dobar dan, ja se zovem Lt. Carraway." That's about it.

But New York was still there after the Armistice, and upon my return I could think of no tempting alternative to trolling in the marts of money. I took a small cottage that summer on Long Island, from which I commuted to a brokerage firm on Wall Street. I wanted to be rich and careless like the people in whose circles I managed to move with diminishing comfort during that summer and autumn in the Twenties; most especially my immediate neighbor and friend, a man named Gatsby. But Gatsby died--was murdered actually--and my romance with a lady golfer soured, and finally I had to face the fact that I was out of my element there.

And so I came back to the Midwest, where I have lived ever since. I tried my hand at a few different careers--my family's hardware business was the first one, but I was no more suited to it than I'd imagined I would be. I wrote a novel drawn from my experiences in the East, which brought me a brief flare of literary success. I parlayed that into a stint as a journalist at the Chicago Tribune, but soon discovered there were men--such as yourself--who were much better at it than I. After that, I took a short fling at the restaurant business, and even, God help me, spent eight months at the selling of used automobiles.

Then a man I had known at Yale struck up a conversation on the golf course one afternoon that led to our opening an advertising shop in Chicago. Advertising was a wide-open field in those days, and through a combination of ignorance and luck we managed to make a pretty good thing of it. Taylor & Carraway today has branches in Minneapolis and Milwaukee in addition to the home office on Fair Street, with billings of over six million.

We even handled a piece of the Eisenhower campaign, and I spent some time with Allen Dulles, whom I had known in France in '18. Dulles asked me if I'd be interested in a stint of government service when Ike took office (he was very confident about that!) Said his brother was in line for State in an Eisenhower administration. I told him I'd think about it, and next thing I knew I had a job in Washington, and a leave of absence from the firm.

So here I am, with an office in Foggy Bottom and not the foggiest idea what I'm doing here, other than trying to do a bit of good in terms of selling the American message abroad and helping the Europeans understand what we're all about. It will be a great help to me if I can mine the brains and experiences of men like you, who have lived abroad long enough to have a European's view of what it is America represents. But I would be dissembling if I didn't add that in your case, the motivation is more personal. As I've said before, I'm a great fan of your writing. I have a copy of A Lost Generation here in my Washington office. And as much as anything else, I'm frankly hoping to take advantage of the cachet of my moment in the halls of power to strike up a correspondence with one of my literary heroes.

This has been more long-winded than I ever intended. If you're still reading at this point, I hope we can start from scratch and keep in touch.

Very Truly Yours,

Nicholas Carraway

Mlle Christine Jorgensen
Royal Hospital
Copenhagen, Denmark

3 February

Dear Jake,

Language, language! Remember, I'm a lady now.

Thanks for your note. Yes, I'm fine. Sore as hell, but fine. More than fine. Wonderful. Terrified, but wonderful. So much to get used to! I keep bursting into tears, and I'm not even unhappy. I'm ecstatically happy. I wish I knew what the hell was going on.

It has been the most extraordinary journey, and I am just now arriving on the shores of an amazing, exotic land. I always assumed, vaguely and romantically, that once I crossed that border, I would be truly at home, and I'd feel at home right away.

And in a way, that's true. My body fits me now, as it never did before. All the parts feel right. But what else fits? I used to love playing dress-up when I was little--drove my Dad crazy. And for the past year or so, as I started trying to prepare myself for this leap into the unknown, I dressed more and more the way I wanted to be. But in a way, it was still playing dress-up.

Now it's real, and it's scarier than
I thought it would be. Now I have to get
it right. Everyone will be looking at me,
looking for any mistake.

But you, Jake. You have demons of
your own, don't you? Despite being the
gruff old bear who walks by himself and
doesn't need anything from anybody. Sew it
back on? What an idea! You're more than
welcome to mine. It may smell a little of
formaldehyde, but ... I wonder!

I'll put you in touch with Dr.
Hamburger.

Warmest Regards,

Christine

Ronnie Gilchrist
Snicklepoo and the Baby Sitter
WGKG Chicago

February 4, 1953

Dear Mr. Carraway,

The strangest thing. I got a letter from
Senator McCarthy's committee asking me to
come and testify. I can't imagine what
they think I can help them with, though of
course, I'll help in any way I can. Do you
know Senator McCarthy?

Congratulations again on your new job. Mr.
Taylor has been wonderful in giving me
advice about the show, but I know it never
would have worked as well as it did without
you. I still have these urges to tinker with
the show, like singing some new songs. There
are some awfully cute ones out now, like
that one about the doggie in the window. And
I was just looking at some darling polka dot
fabric that would make a cute new bowtie for
Snicklepoo, but I keep reminding myself of
what you said about not changing a thing.
Well, you know me. The eternal worry wart.
If I were in Washington, I'd probably be
tinkering with the Constitution and the
Declaration of Independence.

I'll be in Washington at the end of the week. I'll be staying at the YWCA. It would be wonderful to see you while I'm there--and Mrs. C., of course--but I know how busy you must be running the country.

Your friend,

Ronnie Gilchrist

Jacob Barnes
Paris Herald Tribune
38, rue de Berri
Paris 16, France

February 6

Carraway:

Oh, you're <u>that</u> Nicholas Carraway? Yes,
I read your novel about the gangster. It
wasn't as bad a novel as the critics later
made it out to be, but it was a very poor
novel.

Barnes

Jake Barnes
1 rue de Fleurus
Paris 6, France

Feb. 6

Dear George, or I guess it's Mlle. Christine
now?

Don't do anything too fast. I've been
getting the damnedest letters from a State
Department flack named Nicholas Carraway.
Started by asking me about subversive books
in overseas libraries--what the hell is
that all about? These guys think they own
the press. Any pipe dreams we had about Ike
coming in and sweeping the Tail-gunner aside
are looking like hashish now. Especially
with the Dulles Brothers running things.

But Carraway interests me, and I'll tell you
why.

The guy is a writer, or used to be. Wrote
a swell novel about a thousand years ago,
by the name of Trimalchio in West Egg. It
was damn good, well written, and true. He
gave his character an inner honesty that
said more about the best and worst in
America than I ever expected to see from our
godforsaken generation. What's damn ironic,
considering his first letter to me, is that

I ordered a bunch of copies of it when I was in charge of purchasing for the Voice of America.

Anyway, now he's telling me the story of his life. The Reader's Digest condensed version: He sold out.

There's something sad about him, as there is with most sellouts. I wonder if he still has a chance to make it right. There aren't too goddamned many second acts to American lives. Be nice to think his could be one of them.

If not, maybe the second act is another Carraway I just met recently, this one with the first name Alden. Jimmy Baldwin introduced me, so he's probably a queer --fit right in with your velvet mafia in Washington. Just as likely a Red, too. Certainly an idealist. But I liked him. He submitted an article to me for Encounter. Fuzzy thinking, but he can write. I'm sending it on to Kristol, with a recommendation that we publish it. Wonder if the kid's any relation to the State Department Carraway? Wouldn't surprise me. But then nothing surprises me anymore. Fuck it, George--sorry, Chris--Carraway's book was good. He was a damn sight too bowled over by the rich, which is probably why he sold out. Still is, apparently. Made

a point of telling me his agency billed six
fucking million a year.

Well, I'm not telling him I liked his book.
It'd just encourage him. He wants to be
friends, and old Barnyard Jake has all the
friends he needs. I'll keep on being rude to
the poor slob. Maybe he'll go the hell away.
Listen lady, write to me. I want to know how
you're doing with the new plumbing. When are
you going to be up and around?

Yr Man of Mystery,

Jake

MEMORANDUM

2/6/53
Memo from: Jake Barnes
To: Irving Kristol

Sending along a manuscript by a kid who's
been bombarding me with them. Name's Alden
Carraway. Raw, simple prose, and a nodding
acquaintance with truth. Reminds me of me
when I was younger, only I got over it.
He's got this idea that the personal is
the political and vice versa. Naive, but
provocative. Hope you like it, you goddamned
cynic.

He's in a lather over the situation in
Iran. He's been hanging out with some
expat Persians in the Latin Quarter, and
he's fallen in love with Mossadegh and
his People's Government over there in
Iran. (Which he seems to think the U.S. is
planning to pull the rug out from under.)
Not sure how solid his information is, but
I'm also not sure he's wrong. I've got some
sources I'm going to shake a little and see
what falls out of the tree.

The kid can write, though. He's come up
with a catchy name for the underdeveloped
countries--he calls them "The Third World."
He uses the term to refer to the unaligned
nations, the ones who're neither in our

net nor the Russkis', and it's got a sly
reference to the Third Estate, the Great
Unwashed of the French Revolution. Not bad,
eh?

Odd coincidence--I've gotten a couple of
letters from another Carraway, a stuffed
shirt in the Eisenhower administration.
Wrote a pretty good novel about a hundred
years ago, name of <u>Trimalchio in West Egg</u>.
Turns out he's the kid's father. Offspring
doesn't think much of the old fart.
Hypocrite, sellout--you know. Wonder what
kids of ours would have to do to rebel?
Become right wing crypto-fascists and
bundists, I guess. That reminds me--I hear
you and Bea are expecting. Congratulations,
I guess.

Barnes

ENCOUNTER
New York, NY

February 10, 1953

Jake,

Thanks for the congratulations, I guess.
I'll read the young lion's manuscript.
Look, don't bother with the Iran thing. I've
heard those rumors too, they're bullshit.
You can hear a dozen others sitting around
the coffee houses and beer halls where the
kids hang out.

Meanwhile, here's something you may find
interesting. This, of course, like so
much correspondence and cocktail party
conversation these days, relates to the
junior senator from Wisconsin. He fills the
lineaments of a thug, sometimes to comic
effect, and this transcript from a recent
hearing may amuse you--especially since it
relates to your pen pal Carraway. It comes
from the testimony of a young lady named
Ronnie Gilchrist, who appears to have the
demeanor (and intellectual capacity) of
a kindergarten teacher. (The underlines
and marginal notes, of course, are mine--
the committee stenographer has no sense of
irony.)

McCarthy: Please state your name for the
            record.

Gilchrist: Veronica Edith Gilchrist.

McCarthy: But that's not the name you use,
             is it?

Gilchrist: People call me Ronnie.

McCarthy: People call you ... ?

Gilchrist: Everybody does. My parents, my
             friends ... it's a nickname.

McCarthy: Come on, Miss Gilbert. Isn't
             it a fact ... isn't it a fact
             that you hide behind this alias,
             as if you have been deliberately
             trying to hide your true
             identity?

(You've got to read it with that flat
Midwestern twang of his--isn't it a fact ...
isn't it a fact ... priceless!)

Gilchrist: No, I just ... Ronnie just seems
             friendlier ...

McCarthy: Friendlier? Are you telling this
             committee that you desire to be
             friendly?

Gilchrist: Well, yes, of course.

McCarthy: Friendly as in a friendly witness
             for the committee, or friendly as

in ... Comrade?

Gilchrist: Huh?

Cohn: Mr. Chairman, the witness is being unresponsive.

McCarthy: Witness is directed to answer the question.

McCarthy: Never mind. I think we can all figure out the answer. Miss Gilbert ... Miss so-called <u>Ronnie</u> Gilbert--I hand you this piece of paper and ask you to read the words on it.

Gilchrist: (reading) I was at Franklin Roosevelt's side / Just a while before he died / He said, "One world must come out of World War II, / Yankee, Russian, white or tan, / Lord, a man is just a man, / We're all brothers and we're only passing through." ... Oh, now I understand ...

McCarthy: You understand? You understand this dirty, Communistic, unpatriotic piece of Red garbage? Well, that's very interesting, <u>Ronnie</u>, because most Americans ... most <u>real</u> Americans ...

would not understand such a piece of <u>verminous treason</u>.

(My God, <u>verminous</u>--don't you love it?)

Gilchrist: No ... I meant ... I understand how you got confused. This is a song by the Weavers--"Passing Through." The girl in the Weavers is Ronnie Gilbert. I'm Ronnie Gilchrist.

McCarthy: Are you trying to tell the committee that you don't know the words to this song?

Gilchrist: Oh, yes. We used to sing it at camp. We never sang that verse, though.

McCarthy: What are some of the verses you did sing at this indoctrination camp?

Gilchrist: (starting to cry) It was Girl Scout camp!

Cohn: Mr. Chairman, the witness is being unresponsive.

McCarthy: Witness is directed to answer the question.

Gilchrist: What ...

McCarthy: I'll repeat the question, since
            you appear to have one of those
            convenient memory lapses that
            happen so often to Communists
            and fellow travelers. You tell
            the committee you do know the
            words to this Commie filth? Recite
            them for us. You ... heh-heh ...
            you don't have to <u>sing</u> ...

(Appreciative ripple of laughter from the
gallery. The guy can work a crowd!)

Gilchrist: Well, it starts "I was with
            George Washington ... "

McCarthy: I want it noted in the record
            that these Commies will stop
            at nothing to infiltrate our great
            American patriotic heritage. Miss
            Gilbert ...

Gilchrist: (in a squeaky whisper) Gilchrist.

McCarthy: Miss Gilbert, what are the names
            of your pals in this so-called
            singing group, the Weavers?

Gilchrist: Their names?

(Committee Counsel Roy Cohn whispers to Sen.
McCarthy. I don't know about that Cohn--smart
as hell, but a weasel.)

McCarthy: Is there some reason why you
              don't want to tell us their
              names?

Gilchrist: No, of course not. I want to help
              the committee. But I'm not ...

McCarthy: You say you want to help the
              Committee. But you refuse to give
              us their names?

Gilchrist: No ... I ... let's see ...
              there's Pete Seeger ...

(Cohn whispers.)

McCarthy: The well-known Communist.

Gilchrist: And Lee Hays ...

(And Cohn again.)

McCarthy: The well-known Communist.

Gilchrist: And Ronnie Gilbert ... and I
              can't remember the other.

McCarthy: Come on now, Ronnie.

Gilchrist: (sobbing) I ...

McCarthy: Come on. You're doing fine.
              This Committee wants to believe

you. This Committee is here to
help you and all patriotic
Americans. We know there are
a lot of fellow travelers like
you who've seen the light, and
are now ready to defend America.
What about you, Ronnie? Do you
want to help defend America?

Gilchrist: Yes ... oh, yes!

McCarthy: Yes, what?

Gilchrist: I want to help defend America.

McCarthy: Okay, then. You've given us this
             Seeger. Good. You've given us
             this Hays. Good. Why do you
             continue to refuse to give us the
             other name?

Gilchrist: (still sobbing) I can't ... I
             can't remember!

(Cohn again.)

(And again.)

McCarthy: Well, don't worry, sister. We'll
             get to the bottom of this. I
             have no more questions of this
             witness, Mr. Chairman. I think
             it's pretty clear where she
             stands.

Gilchrist: No! No! I'm a good American!
             I hate the Communists! I
             ... I ... I know somebody in
             President Eisenhower's
             administration!

McCarthy: And who would this be, Miss
             Gilbert?

Gilchrist: Mr. Nicholas Carraway--he's in
the   State Department!

(Silence in the room. A long whispered
conference between Cohn and McCarthy. Notes
are written down.)

McCarthy: Request a subpoena be issued
             in the name of Mr. Nicholas
             Carraway.

(ENCRYPTED AND DECODED)
(2/10)

FROM: IRVING KRISTOL
TO: ALLEN DULLES

BARNES MAKING NOISES ABOUT NOSING INTO IRAN.
I'VE LAUGHED HIM OFF IT, BUT HE COULD MAKE
TROUBLE.

--KRISTOL

(ENCRYPTED AND DECODED)
(2/11)

FROM: ALLEN DULLES
TO: IRVING KRISTOL
TOP SECRET

BE CAREFUL WITH BARNES. HE SMELLS SOMETHING,
AND I'M NOT READY TO TAKE A CHANCE ON
BRINGING HIM INTO THIS YET. HE'S SMART, SO
WATCH YOUR STEP. ENCOUNTER IS A KEY PART OF
OPERATION ELBA. WE HAVE THE NATIONAL STUDENT
ASSOCIATION COVERED, AND BETWEEN THAT AND
ENCOUNTER WE CAN STIR UP TROUBLE, AND KEEP
MONITORING IT AT THE SAME TIME.

IF WE KEEP ENOUGH LEFTIST AGITATION GOING
IN FRANCE, THAT'LL KEEP THE RIGHT CHASING
THEIR TAILS, WHICH MEANS NO CHANCE OF A

STABLE GOVERNMENT. WHICH MEANS NO ONE TO
KEEP A HANDLE ON THE WAR IN INDO-CHINA.
THE COMMUNIST THREAT WILL START TO MAKE
AMERICANS NERVOUS, BUT IT WON'T REALLY
HAPPEN UNTIL AFTER IKE'S WOUND UP TWO TERMS,
AND A DEMOCRAT GETS IN.

THE DEMOCRATS INHERIT A QUAGMIRE, AND BY
1964, YOUR NEOCONSERVATIVE COUNTERREVOLUTION
SHOULD HAVE ALL ITS DUCKS LINED UP, AND WE
CAN SWEEP INTO POWER BEHIND NIXON. IF NIXON
SELF-DESTRUCTS, WE MIGHT LOOK AT THAT GUY
FROM ARIZONA, GOLDWATER.

IT'S A FOOLPROOF PLAN. AND IF THE DEMOCRATIC
PRESIDENT TURNS OUT TO BE TOO POPULAR (BUT I
FIGURE IT'LL BE HARRIMAN, SO THAT'S NOT TOO
LIKELY) ... WELL, THERE ARE WAYS OF DEALING
WITH THAT, TOO.

SO, FOR NOW, STAY IN PLACE. AS FOR THE
POSITION YOU SHOULD BE TAKING ON IRAN, PRO-
MOSSADEGH, ALL THE WAY. WE DON'T WANT TO TIP
OUR HAND THAT WE'RE EVEN CONSIDERING ANOTHER
OPTION. SO DON'T WORRY ABOUT PUBLISHING
WOOLLY HEADED YOUNG LEFTIES--THAT WORKS
PERFECTLY. REMEMBER, WE'RE BUILDING A WORLD
IN WHICH OUR KIDS WILL CALL THE SHOTS.

DULLES

Jacob Barnes
Paris Herald Tribune
38, rue de Berri
Paris 16, France

Feb. 13

Carraway--

I knew a Jimmy Gatz, back in Kansas City
when I was a cub reporter. He was collecting
for a loan shark. I used him as a source a
few times. He talked more than he should
have, and I thought he was too much of
a dreamer to make it in the rackets. I
wondered what had happened to him. You
got some things wrong about him, but I
recognized the Jimmy I knew in your Gatsby
character.

So what do you want to know about the
International Red Menace?

Barnes

FROM THE DESK OF:
ALLEN DULLES

By special courier
Feb. 15, 1953

Carraway--

So--Barnes is nibbling. Good work. Good
work. For the time being, just play out the
line. Concentrate on strengthening your ties
with the man. Get into his confidence. We
can reel him in later.

Dulles

Nicholas Carraway
Assistant Undersecretary of State for
European Affairs
Department of State
Washington, DC.

February 17, 1953

Dear Mr. Barnes,

So you knew Gatz? I don't wonder you feel I
got some things wrong about him. I no longer
remember what was Gatz and what was Gatsby
and what was just my youthful romantic
imagination.

Don't worry about the libraries. As I said,
I'm just learning this job, and I've been
sending out a lot of letters inherited from
my predecessors. But Lord knows the Red
Menace is real enough, as you should know,
being cheek to jowl over there with the
countries that have been closed off by the
Iron Curtain.

I've been called to testify this week at
the McCarthy hearings. A friendly witness,
they assure me. As I have every intention
of being. My cordial invitation bears
the personal signature of Roy Cohn, the
Chairman's right hand. While I wouldn't
deny that the senator has a touch of the

bull in the china shop to him at times, I'm
sure his intentions are patriotic. Liberals
like to paint him as a fanatical clown, but
there <u>are</u> Communists, Barnes, and they <u>are</u> a
threat to the security of this country. One
of these days I hope I can try to convince
you of that over a martini on the Champs
Elysees.

Meanwhile, I'll wander over to the Hill on
Thursday and see what the committee wants to
talk to me about, and be what help I can.

Yours Truly,

Nick Carraway

New York Herald Tribune

PARIS EDITION, FEBRUARY 17, 1953

THE BARNES DOOR

PARIS--When Dr. Mohammed Mossadegh was elected Premier of Iran, the first thing he did was nationalize his country's oil industry. There may be easier ways of sorting out your friends from your enemies, but this one did the job.

The Iranians thought it was a fine idea. The oil, after all, was Iranian. But the British cried foul. The oil companies, after all, were British. The oil fields might belong to Iran, but the drills and the pumps had John Bull's name tags on them. His Majesty's government sued. The Brits took the matter to the United Nations. Dr. Mossadegh went to New York and won his case before the Security Council. Then he went to The Hague to defend the takeover, and he won again in the World Court.

Dr. Mossadegh stopped in Paris on his way home from the Netherlands, and he sat down for a few minutes with this newspaper. He is a quiet, frail man, who projects the aggrieved air of a beagle hound shut up in a hot car. But when he talks about his country, his eyes light up, and he leans forward like a preacher in his pulpit.

"Democracy is possible in the Middle East," he said. "It is as your Mr. Jefferson put it so eloquently, there comes a time in the course of human events when it becomes necessary for one people to dissolve the political bands which have connected them with another ... "

Nobody likes to lose something they think of as their own. From time to time whispers reach us of plans for a British invasion of Iran, which seems unlikely. We've also heard rumors of a coup sponsored by Britain. That sounds more plausible. But Dr. Mossadegh enjoys the backing of something like 98 percent of the people of his country, so a popular uprising against him may be a hard story to sell.

Where did Dr. Mossadegh get a crazy idea like nationalizing the oil industry? He says he got it from the British.

"They are nationalizing their steel industry," he pointed out, "and their railroads. They tell us it is different for them, that they are an advanced civilization. My ancestors were civilized when Winston Churchill's ancestors wore skins and lived in caves. My only crime is that I removed from this land the network of colonialism and the political and economic influence of the greatest empire on earth."

Some of the whispers that have reached us have the British looking to America for help with their problem. What business is it of ours? It isn't. If anybody tells you it is, tell him to look up what America stands for. We stand up for the little guy. We stand up for the poor, the downtrodden, the huddled masses yearning to breathe free. Undercutting democracy is not America's style. Never has been, and please God, never will be. We leave empire to the empire-builders, and colonialism to the colonialists.

ENCOUNTER
New York, NY

Irving Kristol
February 20

Well, Barnes, I just read through the latest
transcripts from the McCarthy hearings, and
your friend Carraway seems to have run into
a Mack truck at the committee. Enclosed is
the truck. You'll enjoy this exchange with
the junior senator from Wisconsin.

McCarthy: Mr. Carraway, I, uh ... Mr.
             Carraway, will you tell this
             committee how you were employed
             before you came to the State
             Department?

Carraway: Certainly, Senator. I am a
             partner in the advertising firm
             of Taylor and Carraway, based in
             Chicago. We've got an office up
             in your neck of the woods, too--
             Milwaukee. I'm on leave from
             that outfit right now, and I
             hope they won't change the locks
             on me while I spend a little time
             working for the government.

McCarthy: (laughs) I'm sure they won't.
             Mr. Carraway ... do you employ
             any known Communists at your

advertising firm?

Carraway: No sir, I do not.

McCarthy: None at all, Mr. Carraway? Are you quite sure of that?

Carraway: Of course I am. Do you have evidence that I am mistaken?

McCarthy: We'll have no more of that, Mr. Carraway. You will answer the question.

Carraway: Senator, I'm here at the committee's invitation, and I mean to help in any way I can.

McCarthy: I, uh ... I think it might be better for you, Carraway, if you just came out with it yourself. That is, if you don't have anything to hide ...

Carraway: With all due respect, Senator, I am being as responsive as I possibly can.

McCarthy: In other words, Carraway, you refuse to tell this committee about the Reds you do business with in this little advertising game of yours?

Carraway: Damn it, Senator, stop your
             insinuations! If you have
             something to say, say it!

Cohn: (whispering) He's covering
             up, like they all do. Hit him
             with the testimony.

(Roy Cohn hands a document to Sen.
McCarthy.)

McCarthy: I show you the testimony of a
             young woman in the entertainment
             business, a well-known Communist
             named Ronnie Gilbert, who names
             you as a close associate ...

Carraway: Ronnie Gil ... oh, you mean
             Ronnie Gilchrist. Sure, she's a
             good kid. She does a children's
             show for us. A Communist?
             Senator, I don't know who does
             your investigating, but if it's
             Mr. Cohn, I suggest you take away
             his Junior G-Man kit.

(Cohn turns a lovely shade of red, something
on the order of a '47 Margaux.)

Cohn: Look here, Carraway ...

McCarthy: Mr. Carraway, Mr. Cohn is our chief counsel, and he is entitled to normal courtesy.

Caraway: My apologies, Mr. Cohn.

McCarthy: What about this little Red thrush, Nick? Did you ever ask her if she was a Communist?

Carraway: No.

McCarthy: Weren't you curious? If somebody told me an associate of mine was a Communist, I'd get on the phone and say, 'What about this? Is this true?'

Carraway: Nobody ever told me she was a Communist! Senator, that little girl hasn't got a political bone in her body. She's about as subversive as Snow White!

McCarthy: Nick, we're going to give you a chance to redeem yourself here. Can you tell us, of your own knowledge, about anyone else, in or out of government, who may have had trysts with this little Red thrush, from whom she may have extracted information that could be useful to the enemies of our country?

Carraway: No! Damn it, McCarthy ...

McCarthy: Let me shift to another line of
            questioning, Nickie. Would you
            like to tell this committee about
            your associations with known
            gangsters?

Carraway: I ... what?

McCarthy: Oh, come on, Carraway. Meyer
            Wolfsheim? Does that name ring
            any bells? James Gatz?

Well, those are the highlights. The Daily
Mirror ran a story under the headline,
TOP IKE MAN IN LOVE NEST WITH "LITTLE RED
THRUSH." I don't know about the thrush, but
where there's smoke, there's fire. You can
forget Carraway. He won't be playing you the
National Anthem any more. He's as washed up
as last week's laundry.

Kristol

From the desk of:
JOHN FOSTER DULLES

February 20, 1953

Mr. Carraway,

As you know, we expect those in whom
President Eisenhower places his trust to
be completely forthcoming about their
associations. Senator McCarthy has raised
serious questions about yours. The State
Department wishes to be fair, but we will
need to see a much fuller explanation from
you.

Yours truly,

John Foster Dulles
Secretary of State

Mrs. Nicholas Carraway
40125 Oak Park Drive
Oak Park, Illinois

February 21, 1953

Nicholas,

I've always had my suspicions about you and your little Red thrush. I'm only amazed that you thought you could pull the wool over the eyes of a man like Senator McCarthy.

A woman has a right to expect a man who'll take care of her and put her on a pedestal, just the way our country has a right to expect people to honor her values and our American way of life. Well, I'm keeping the house, and the car, and all our possessions. I deserve them.

A locksmith is here today, changing the locks on all of the doors, and installing an alarm system. It used to be safe to leave your door unlocked in this town. No more. Children used to respect their elders. You used to be able to walk down the street, and every kid you saw, you knew who their family was, and they'd tip their caps or give a little curtsey, just as if the whole village was part of bringing them up. But that's another thing the damn Communists have taken away from us.

I knew when I married you that you had
"artistic" tendencies--that silly book--
but I let myself believe you had put it
all behind you. I suppose love is blind. I
should have seen it all along. The way our
son has turned into a wild-eyed Bohemian
just breaks my heart. Certainly Alden didn't
take after my side of the family. The Pyles
are decent stock.

I don't understand how General Eisenhower
could have appointed a man like you to
a position of influence. Senator Taft
never would have done it. I never trusted
Eisenhower. You do know how cozy he was with
the Russians during the war. Well, I believe
the country is coming to its senses, and
Senator McCarthy will be our next president.
From now on, you may direct all contact with
me to my lawyers, Quayle and Quayle.

With no affection,

Margery Carraway

A NEW YORK JOURNAL AMERICAN EXCLUSIVE

by DOROTHY KILGALLEN

February 22, 1953

STATE DEPT. PINKO, LITTLE RED THRUSH IN CONSPIRACY

This reporter has learned of a secret correspondence between "Little Red Thrush" Ronnie Gilbert and Nicholas Carraway, the State Department Commie recently unmasked by the McCarthy Committee. We have obtained a copy of a letter in which the Thrush tells Pinko Nicko, "If I were in Washington, I'd probably be tinkering with the Constitution and the Declaration of Independence."

From the desk of:

JOHN FOSTER DULLES

February 23, 1953

Mr. Carraway:

I expect your letter of resignation on my
desk by 5:00 PM today.

John F. Dulles

Secretary of State

Nicholas Carraway
c/o YMCA
1711 Rhode Island Avenue NW
Washington, DC

Feb. 26

Dear Margery,

After all the catastrophic events of the
last ten days, your bombshell is neither the
most unexpected nor, if truth be told, the
most wounding. If we are both honest, we'll
admit that this breakup has been a long time
coming. Our marriage has been an abandoned
battlefield for many years now.

I don't think we need to quarrel over the
division of spoils. I shan't want much. I
have enough clothes here in Washington.
I've instructed Dick Daley to sort out the
money and property and to make sure you have
everything you need and want.

As for my "Little Red Thrush," as you and
the press and that idiot McCarthy delight
in calling Miss Gilchrist, she is as
innocent in all this as a songbird struck
by a speeding train. The idea of my having
had an affair with that young lady would
be laughable if the effect of all this
weren't so tragic. She has, I would guess,

less knowledge of sex than you do. That
our conjugal life managed to produce a son
proves, I think, the existence if not of
Divine Miracles then at least of a Cosmic
Sense of Humor.

My immediate plans are vague. I only know
that they call for putting an ocean between
me and the country that until a week ago I
served without reservation. I still believe
in this country, but at the moment the
evidence suggests that it does not think
much of me.

If you should have any reason to get in
touch with me, you can write care of the
Guarantee Trust Co. in Paris. I'm going to
try to find Alden and see what I can do
about making up for things.

A good marriage is a terrible thing to
waste. Ours, however, is one the world will
little note, nor long remember.

Yours, Nick

(ENCRYPTED AND DECODED)
(2/24)
FROM: IRVING KRISTOL
TO: ALLEN DULLES

DO WE NEED SOMEONE ELSE TO SHADOW BARNES?
IT LOOKS AS THOUGH CARRAWAY'S OUT OF THE
PICTURE. OR ARE YOU WORKING WITH MCCARTHY ON
THIS?

KRISTOL

(ENCRYPTED AND DECODED)
(2/25)
FROM: ALLEN DULLES
TO: IRVING KRISTOL

WORK WITH MCCARTHY? IT WOULD BE EASIER TO
WORK WITH GARGANTUA. BUT MCCARTHY CAN BE A
USEFUL IDIOT. HE'S DROPPED A GIFT INTO OUR
LAP RE: OPERATION ELBA WITH THIS CARRAWAY
BUSINESS. IT'S A PERFECT COVER FOR C. TO
INGRATIATE HIMSELF WITH THE LEFTIES. RIGHT
NOW HE'S FEELING LIKE A SAFE FELL ON HIM.
WE'LL LET HIM LICK HIS WOUNDS ON HIS OWN, TO
KEEP HIM CONVINCING, BEFORE WE BRING HIM IN
AND BRIEF HIM. BUT HE'S A COMPANY MAN. HE'LL
PLAY BALL.

DULLES

Mr. Alden Carraway
C/o American Embassy
Paris

Dear Alden,

I'm sure you'll have heard by now about
your father and the McCarthy hearings. I
still don't understand it. You'd think a
man who had served his country and his
family with such conspicuous colorlessness
would be spared the indignity of these
wild accusations of love nests, Communist
conspiracy, and high treason.

I'm on board the Ile de France, sailing for
Paris. Right now I have an overwhelming need
to get away, not just from Washington, but
from everything familiar. It's not so much
that I am feeling the disgrace. For some
curious reason that doesn't seem to bother
me as much as it should. Men I've known for
years are suddenly crossing the street to
avoid me, and somehow I find the uncrowded
side of the street much more agreeable
than I would have thought. I have more the
sensation of going toward something than
running away.

We'll have a good talk when I see you, which I hope will be soon. I will be staying at the George V, and I hope to be able to buy you dinner and begin a long and very important process of making things right between us.

Your Loving Father

PS. Your mother and I have separated.

FROM: NICHOLAS CARRAWAY
ABOARD THE ILE DE FRANCE D T
TO: JACOB BARNES, PARIS HERALD TRIBUNE
3/3/53

ARRIVING PARIS THURSDAY UNDER CLOUD STOP
IF STILL SPEAKING TO PARIAH CONTACT HOTEL
GEORGE V
CARRAWAY

Alden Carraway
219 rue de Vaugirard
Paris 15th

3 March

Dear Mr. Barnes,

It has been a while since you've heard from me and had to deal with my submissions to Encounter. You were kind enough to take me seriously and give me some encouragement, and for that I'm very grateful.

I just wanted to let you know that I'm leaving Paris, and it will probably be a while before I try writing anything for publication again. I met an amazing guy at the Dome a couple of weeks ago, an American named Larry Darrell. I don't know how to describe him to you--he was kind of bohemian in his dress, with a threadbare coat patched at the elbows, no hat or tie. His hair needed cutting, and he wore a full beard that showed signs of gray. But his smile was dazzling--white, even teeth, and dark eyes that seemed to start somewhere way back deep in his head. There was a look in those eyes that I can't explain, except to say that you felt like they knew something, or very likely everything.

We got to talking. I told him I was a writer. He listened to me spout my ideas

about politics and social inequality, and he
didn't say much, but I had the feeling that
my words were being drawn into some profound
and infinite space, as if he were not just
hearing me but absorbing me into something
universal. I know this will sound ridiculous
to you, Mr. Barnes, but I was impressed
and a bit unsettled. I realized that I was
talking to someone who had actually been to
the places I was only writing about. What
did I know about the "Third World"? What was
I doing, trying to tell anyone else about
it?

We met again a few days later, and he told
me a bit about himself, about how as a young
man he had traveled to India and spent some
time in an "ashram" there. He'd achieved
something he called enlightenment, which
I don't begin to understand, but I can
tell you that the effect it seems to have
produced in him is something we all could
use a bit of.

Anyway, I've decided to give up writing and
Paris and political causes for the time
being, and head East to see if I can find
some of this enlightenment stuff for myself.
I don't know where exactly this search will
take me, but I'll try to keep in touch
and let you know how I'm doing. Again, I
appreciate all your help and belief in me.

Yours Truly,

Alden Carraway

PS. Apparently my father is coming to Paris.
That's another reason I'm taking off.

Hotel George V
MESSAGE
EN VOTRE ABSENCE

March 5

Pour M. Carraway
De la part de M. Barnes

Carraway —

Jesus, what the hell are you thinking? You can't afford this place. I hope to Christ you haven't checked in already. The George fucking Sank? This is the Fifties, Carraway, not the Twenties, and they charge real money these days. I read the papers, I know your assets are tied up tighter than a priest's vasectomy. Make your excuses and get a cab. There's a swell little joint on the Rue St. Sulpice, across the river; not too bad if you don't need to extend your arms. Tell the driver Hotel de l'Odeon. They know me there. I booked you a room on the second floor — that's the first floor over here — it'll save hauling your luggage up more than one flight of stairs. Bienvenue a Paris. I'll call you tomorrow.

— Barnes

Jake Barnes
1 rue de Fleurus
Paris 6, France

Dear Chris,

Carraway going, Carraway coming. Young Alden
writes to tell me he's chucking politics for
enlightenment. He met up with Larry Darrell
--you know, the chap who started Brett off
on Eastern thought--and there went another
young firebrand out to change the world.
Perhaps it's all for the best. Who the hell
knows.

I've met Darrell. He's good. He's very good.
And sometimes the damn world does seem
vanity of vanities, like the prophet says.
The wind goeth toward the south, and turneth
again to the north. The King Barnes version
of the Good Book--product of a misspent
youth. It's all horseshit, anyway--I don't
know whether I give a damn what people
believe in--but it matters to me that people
have the guts to stand guard in a lonely
outpost of the maquis, or to keep secrets
for strangers they'll never see again.
Who's to say Alden's wrong? But I keep
punching anyway, against the bastards.
Whoever they are.

Meanwhile, the father has arrived in Paris.
Nick Carraway, who I told you about. Poor
guy has had his belief system shot out from
under him. The American Dream, Eisenhower
edition, marginal notes by Tailgunner Joe
McCarthy. I know how he feels, having been
shot up a bit myself.

We're a fuckingly complicated generation,
Chris--ripped untimely from the womb of
innocence and thrust into a meat grinder.
Hard to imagine if you weren't there. You've
made a hell of an Odyssey, but going to
Denmark was the smallest part of it. For
us--me, Carraway, Darrell--leaving America
was probably the biggest part. Those of us
who never went back, it turns out we could
never really leave it. Guys like Carraway
who tried to go back, never really got
there. It's all tied up with Einstein and
relativity--you can't step in the same river
twice. How's that for irony and pity?

Je t'embrasse,

Jake

Ronnie Gilchrist
1337 Primrose Lane
Winnetka, Illinois

Mr. Nicholas Carraway
C/O Guarantee Trust Co., Paris, France
March 10, 1953

Dear Mr. Carraway,

First of all, I'm so sorry for everything
that's happened to you. I guess I just don't
understand what can be going on in America
if a man like you is accused of being un-
American. My mother says where there's smoke
there's fire, and I keep trying to tell her
that Senator McCarthy said some terrible
things about me, too, but she just pretends
she's not listening. When I tell her that I
lost my TV show because of it, she says that
was all your fault. But I know that's not
true. I know you're the finest man I ever
met, and if America has turned its back on
you, well, there must be something wrong
with America, that's all I can say.

So much has happened since I last wrote you,
and some of it's been exciting, but it's all
left me very confused. I'm not sure what to
do, and I wondered if I could turn to you
for advice. After I left Washington, and
came back to Winnetka, I got a call from Mr.
Irving Sheinbloom in New York!!!!! If you

don't know who he is, he's a major figure in
the Folk Music field! He wants me to come
to New York and talk to him, he says he has
some wonderful ideas for a new career for
me. I told him that I was afraid no one
wanted to hear so much as my name any more,
but he said that in New York that would all
be different.

I hope you don't mind me writing to you,
after all that's happened. If you do,
just tell me Ronnie, go away, and I'll
understand. I do feel so terrible knowing it
was me who dragged your name into this.
I hope you're liking France. I would love to
go to France or Europe one day.

Your Friend,

Ronnie Gilchrist

4/12/53

FROM: I. KRISTOL
ENCOUNTER MAGAZINE, NY

TO: LAWRENCE DARRELL
POSTE RESTANTE
LHASA, TIBET

DARRELL
HOW ARTICLE ON INDOCHINA COMING?

KRISTOL

4/12/53

FROM: LAWRENCE DARRELL
POSTE RESTANTE
LHASA, TIBET

TO: ALLEN DULLES
CENTRAL INTELLIGENCE AGENCY
WASHINGTON, DC

DULLES--
MAY HAVE SOMEONE FOR YOU

DARRELL

Nicholas Carraway
Hotel de l'Odeon
14 March 1953

Dear Miss Gilchrist,

Please don't think of trying to shoulder the
blame for this sorry turn of events. I'm
afraid your mother is right--if anyone is
to blame, I am. It was my responsibility to
protect you. Unfortunately, I couldn't even
help myself, so here we both are, orphans of
the storm.

I'm glad to hear that you are finding some
opportunities in the folk music field.
You do want to be careful, though. I get
the impression that real Communists do
actually lurk behind the guitars and banjos
of the "hootenanny" stage. Although, to be
perfectly honest, I really know very little
about the subject.

That seems to be my essential truth these
days--I'm coming to realize that I know
precious little about much of anything. When
your country sucker punches you, it knocks
you for a loop. I'm sure you feel that too,
but in my case there is another quarter-
century or so of accumulated beliefs and
assumptions to eat, and it leaves a bitter
taste in the mouth and a hollow pain in the
belly.

(I had delusions of being a writer in my younger days, and you will notice the symptoms rising to the surface from time to time. I'll do my best to contain them.)

So far I have had no luck in one of my objectives in coming to Paris, which was to patch things up with my son Alden. We had a falling out a few years ago, when he accused me of being a prig and stuck in the 19th century. I took offense at the time, but I'm starting to suspect he may have even given me the benefit of a century or two.

I have been here for a week now, and I'm already beginning to feel at home here in a way I never did in Washington. I've made a friend in Jake Barnes, a veteran American journalist who is the Bureau Chief for the Paris Herald Tribune. He's easing my way into the expatriate community. He's a wonderful guy, big and bearded and full of life. And he's that rare bird, or rare in the circles I move in, a man with a conscience to match his intelligence. He actually sees the world in terms of right and wrong. You don't get much of that in Washington. Or even in Chicago, come to think of it.

He warned me off the expensive luxury of the Hotel George V, and arranged my move to a little dive on the Left Bank where I'm now in residence. It's an odd, narrow building

that is said to date to the 16th century.
I can well believe the plumbing hasn't
changed since then, and the room is not much
bigger than a closet, but there is a little
wrought-iron balcony overlooking a pleasant
little courtyard, and the price is right.
The food is great, the wine is cheap, and
the coffee is so good they have a different
word for it over here, "café." But then
they have a different word for everything.
That's the French for you. And there's a bar
called Harry's where they know how to make a
martini that can make a man forget McCarthy.

Please do keep writing, and let me know how
you're doing. I will feel much better about
things if I know you've managed to land on
your feet.

Yours Truly,

Nicholas Carraway

Ronnie Gilchrist
Martha Washington Hotel
New York City

March 19

Dear Mr. Carraway,

Thank you so much for responding to my
letter. It means a lot to me that we can
still be friends. And I just want to tell
you that I LOVE the way you write, and if
I could write like you do, that's what I'd
want to do all the time.

Well, to make a long story short, Mr.
Sheinbloom was calling about The Weavers!
Have you ever heard of them? They're the
folk music group Senator McCarthy was asking
me about? They had that big hit song,
"Goodnight Irene"? Anyway, he's an executive
at Decca Records, and he manages them or
something. He said he'd seen a kinny (sp.?)
of me playing the banjo on "Snicklepoo"
and he wanted me to come and audition
for them!!!!! He said he'd pay my way to
New York. So I decided to come, I mean I
couldn't just sit around in Winnetka and
listen to my mother.

Still, I was scared to death!!! Luckily I
met this nice girl at the Martha Washington

Hotel for Women, where I'm staying. Her
name is Jackie Susann and she wants to be
a writer, and she gave me a pill to calm
my nerves. I'm not sure what it was, but
it really helped when I went in to see Mr.
Sheinbloom. He told me that Mr. Seeger, who
is one of the ones that started the group,
might have to leave because of "trouble
with the government," and they might need
a replacement. I said "But I'm a girl!",
and he just laughed and patted my knee and
said he knew that--isn't that funny? And he
wanted me to come in and meet the Weavers
the next day!

You'll never guess who I got a call from
that night!!!! Do you remember little Johnny
Phillips, one of the Snicklekids on my very
first show? He's a teenager now, and I
guess he's in the mailroom or something at
Decca Records. Anyway he'd heard about me
auditioning for The Weavers, and he wanted
me to show them some arrangements he'd been
working on. He has all these ideas for four-
part harmonies with two men and two girls.
They're a little weird, I guess, but they
sounded really good to me, or maybe it was
just those pills Jackie gave me. Johnny was
so sweet, he said I'd been sort of like a
mama to him, and I was a bit embarrassed,
but I told him we all need mamas and papas.

Anyway, when I got into Mr. Sheinbloom's
office the next morning--that was this
morning, it all just happened!--the Weavers
were all there, except for Mr. Seeger. There
was Mr. Lee Hays, who is this big teddy
bear, so cute. And Ronnie Gilbert--she's the
one who has a name that sounds like mine,
that made Senator McCarthy so mixed up. And
there's another one, they introduced me to
him too, but I can't remember his name now.
I guess I was too nervous. I tried to show
them Johnny's arrangements, but Mr. Hays
laughed and said they don't read music! He
told me to just sing some songs that I knew.
So I sang "John Jacob Jingleheimer Smith,"
and Mr. Hays joined in on the chorus, but
the others didn't seem to like it much. Then
I tried "Hi, Said the Little Leatherwinged
Bat," and they all joined in on the "Howdy,
dowdy" part! I thought it sounded really
good, and Mr. Hays clapped when I played my
banjo break!

Then I wanted to show them that I knew
topical songs like they sang, so I did "The
Ballad of Rodger Young." It's that wonderful
sad song about a private in the infantry
who "fought and died for the men he marched
among." When I finished, Miss Gilbert kind
of stared at me, and the other man said he
was going to go get some fresh air, and Mr.
Hays took Mr. Sheinbloom aside, and Mr. S.
told me to go back to the hotel and he'd

talk to me later. When he called he said it wasn't going to work out with The Weavers, but he's invited me to come up to his apartment this weekend to work with me on some new material. He's so nice!

But here's where I need your advice. He wants to bill me as "The Little Red Thrush." I'm worried it will remind people of Senator McCarthy's committee. What do you think? I can't go back to Winnetka.

Hoping all is well with you.

Your friend,

Ronnie Gilchrist

Roy M. Cohn, Esq.
Office of the Hon. Joseph McCarthy
Senate Office Building
Washington, DC

March 20, 1953

Davey,

It looks good for the Senator being able
to keep you out of the draft. But we need
to make sure that the world knows you're
an important part of the Senator's crusade
against the Communist Menace. I'm thinking
of a fact-finding trip to Europe, which will
give us high visibility (at least in the
daytime). What facts, you ask? I don't know,
but we'll find some!

Anyway, haven't I been promising you we'd
take a vacation, just the two of us? The
Europeans are a bunch of immoral pigs, but
they do have some nice hotels. Don't forget
to pack your purple briefs--you know the
ones I mean. And that torn T-shirt, my
little Stanley Kowalski! Ooh la la!

Love, Daddy

G. David Schine
Hay-Adams Hotel
Washington, DC

Sunday, March 22

Dear Christine,

Congratulations on the operation. But I have
to admit I've got mixt feelings. You were
such a cute <u>boy</u>.

"Daddy" is taking me to Europe! He says
they're a bunch of immorral pigs over
there--I can hardly wait! Not sure where
we'll be--Germinny, I know, and Paris. Have
you got any good French connections? I'd say
let's get together but I don't think so. You
know how jellus "Daddy" gets. (Anyway you're
not my type any more, ha ha!)

Davey

PS. We're looking for REDS. Know any?

Ronnie Gilchrist
Martha Washington Hotel
New York City

March 22

Dear Mr. Carraway,

Just a quick note to tell you something I
overheard last night at Mr. Sheinbloom's
apartment when he was talking on the
phone. That horrid little Mr. Cohn from
the McCarthy Committee is going to Europe
to look for Communists or something. Mr.
Sheinbloom laughed and said, "He should be
able to find some Communists in Europe,
for God's sake. But if he really wanted a
challenge, he'd go to Russia." I'm not sure
where he actually will be going, but I did
hear Mr. S mention Paris, where you are. I
know it has nothing to do with you, but you
be careful just the same. I don't like that
Mr. Cohn!

Mr. S has arranged for me to open for Josh
White at the Village Vanguard next week.
I'm scared to death! But I've been working
like mad, and I have learned some new songs,
like "Last Night I Had the Strangest Dream,"
which is pretty and has a real message.
Mr. S has found an apartment for me on
MacDougal Street, which is right in

Greenwich Village, so I won't be at the
Martha Washington any more. I'll miss Jackie
and the other girls, but Mr. Sheinbloom
says it will be more comfortable and
private having a place of my own. Anyway,
I'm feeling a little funny about the pills
Jackie gives us. I really worry about Carole
Landis and Barbara and especially Judy,
sometimes they're so fun, and then all of
a sudden they just seem to go so ... oh, I
don't know, I guess I'm being silly, and
I know Jackie says there's no harm in the
pills, but maybe I'm better off moving. If
you want to write me, the new address is
Apartment C, 14½ MacDougal Street, New York
12, New York.

I am so nervous about where my career is
going, and this whole "Little Red Thrush"
thing . . . it is the last thing in the
world I ever imagined myself doing, living
in New York City and being a part of the
whole folk music scene. But I don't know
what else to do.

Anyway, you watch out for Mr. Cohn.

Your friend always,

Ronnie

Robert Cohn Associates
1853 M Street NW, Suite 830
Washington, DC

Tuesday, March 24th

Roy,

Attaboy, go get those lousy Commies! And
listen, when you get to France, there's a
son of a bitch in the press corps I'd like
you to stick it to big time. Guy by the name
of Jake Barnes, who I used to know way back
when I was living in Paris. He's arrogant,
thinks he's G-d's gift to women, and I'm
damn sure he's a subversive.

I'm sending a note to my old friend Maurice
Chevalier asking him to show you boys
around when you're in Paris. I think you'll
like Maurice--he's the sort of guy who's
comfortable in any situation. He'll show you
the real Paris, not the one the tourists and
French people see.

Your uncle,

Robert

Robert Cohn Associates
1853 M Street NW, Suite 830
Washington, DC

Tuesday, March 24th

Mon cher Maurice,

My nephew Roy Cohn is coming to Paris on
some business for Senator McCarthy. Maybe
you've heard. He's traveling with a friend,
David Schine. They're bookish boys, and will
be spending a lot of time in libraries. I
want you to see to it that they get out a
bit. Show them a good time. My nephew's
the possessive sort, and I suspect there's
something more than meets the eye to his
interest in his friend. I'd like to try
a little experiment. Lay on the charm,
especially with Schine. You know how to be
charming, don't you, Maurice? I want to
see how Roy reacts when he's hot under the
collar.

My file on you is safe in my cabinet. I
keep it under C, for Collaboration--I mean,
for Chevalier. Thanks Maurice, I know I can
count on you.

Robbie

Nicholas Carraway
Hotel Odeon
Paris

March 26, 1953

Dear Miss Gilchrist,

I apologize for taking so long to get back
to you. Your earlier letter and this one
reached me at the same time. European postal
delivery can be charmingly quirky.
You ask for my advice about Mr. Sheinbloom's
plan to bill you as the Little Red Thrush.

My advice is this: Get back to Winnetka on
the next train! Beware of your friend Jackie
and her pills, and Greenwich Village, and
folk music, and above all Mr. Sheinbloom!
You're a sweet young girl, and there are men
who will take advantage of that.

I appreciate your warning to me to watch
out for Roy Cohn. If he will leave me the
Deux Magots, I am perfectly willing to give
him the rest of Europe. The Deux Magots,
I should tell you, is one of a cluster of
cafés on St. Germain des Prés (others are
called Flore and Lipp and such, but what can
compare with the name Deux Magots!) where
everyone seems to wind up sooner or later.
It is a fascinating place for watching
people.

My instincts about them are almost invariably
wrong. I sat enthralled the other day
watching a craggy fellow dressed in black
velvet, smoking harsh yellow cigarettes,
and scribbling in a notebook. He turned
out to be an insurance salesman totting up
actuarial charts. I paid no attention to
a couple at the next table, a tall woman
made taller by a bun of dark hair piled on
top of her head, and a short, round-faced
man blinking behind owlish spectacles. When
my friend Jake Barnes arrived to join me,
he identified them as the famous writers
and existentialist philosophers, Simone de
Beauvoir and Jean-Paul Sartre!

To my intense mortification, Barnes
introduced me as "Nicholas Carraway, the
American author." Mr. Sartre was very
gracious, and asked me if I knew Nelson
Algren, which seemed to annoy Miss de
Beauvoir. She leaned over and whispered
something to Mr. Sartre. Imagine my surprise
when his face brightened and he said "Ah,
Trimalchio in West Egg!" This is a man who
is probably the most important thinker in
Europe today, and he remembered my book!
My "situation" seems to open more doors than
it closes. McCarthy and his hysteria are
more a joke over here than anything else and
the intellectuals assure us patronizingly
that they don't believe he represents
"les vrais Americains." People are openly

involved with Communism, but nobody gets too worked up about it, considering how much closer they are here to the grim specter of the Iron Curtain.

I am going to love the pace of Paris--the Deux Magots, the afternoon apéritifs with Jake, the sense that the world is both a larger and a more intimate place than I had ever imagined.

Your Friend,

Nick Carraway

Hotel de l'Odeon

Paris

Wednesday

Pour: M. Carraway

De la part de: M. Barnes

Carraway - what was I thinking,
putting you in a place with no telephone?
It's inconvenient as hell leaving these
notes. Get your ass back to the
George fucking Sank, where they've
moved into the goddam 20th century!
Anyway, meet me at the Deux Magots
at 5:30 - I've got some hot poop.
Guess who's heading this way with blood
in his eye and lead in his pencil? Your
old pal Roy Cohn, on a rampage through
Europe with his playmate G David
Schine, in search of god knows what -

one minute they say they're ferreting out
mismanagement and waste in the foreign
information service, the next they're hunting
for subversive literature in USIA libraries
(does that ring a bell?), the next thing
you know they'll be tracking down a
really good liverwurst and a soft pair
of bunny slippers. They landed in
Frankfurt yesterday, and they've got
Paris in their sights. The boys in the
press rooms are agog. This could be the
swellest thing to hit this town since they
invented le strip tease. See you at
dix-sept heures trente — or 5:30,
whichever comes first — and we'll
indulge in some honest drinking and
treasonous ridicule of American
indignitaries.
— Barnes

Hotel Majestic

1 Dong Khoi St
Saigon
Vietnam

27 March

Barnes,

Two-week holiday due me, and I'm on my way
to Paris. You can fill me in on what kind of
awful imperialist lunacy the bloody Yanks
are up to these days. I swear, a few of them
are even starting to filter into Saigon.
Mostly, though, I just want to hit the
nightspots and hear some good American jazz.
I was hoping Philby could get over and join
us for an old-fashioned pub crawl, but our
old chum Kim has funked on us. Busy time at
the Home Office, he claims, Lord knows what
sort of bloody Yank fat to be pulled out of
the fire this time. Thank the bloody heavens
we British have never gone in for this
imperialist nonsense, what?

Hope you appreciate the posh Majestic
stationary. I cribbed some sheets while
I was soaking up a pitcher of their gin
rickeys, the best in Indo-China.

Regards,

Fowler

Hotel D'Angleterre

KONGENS NYTORV 34
COPENHAGEN, DENMARK

3 April

Dear Jake,

Tell me more about your Mr. Carraway.
He interests me. You know I've
always been attracted to men of your
generation--dare I say, without risking
bruised feelings, "older men"? Of
course, I wouldn't ever lump you in with
any generalization. You're my Jake, and
always will be.

This will amuse you. A boy I used to
know, Davey Schine, dropped by to see me
here in Copenhagen. Does the name ring a
bell? He's on a rampage through Europe
with his friend Roy Cohn, Joe McCarthy's
hatchet man. ("Daddy," Davey calls Roy-
-sweet, isn't it?) Perhaps you've run
into them? Apparently they're kicking
up quite a ruckus in your neck of the
woods.

I met Davey and Roy through Clyde
Tolson and his friend, He Who Must Not
Be Named, back when I was exploring the
conventionally unconventional avenues of
sexuality. Davey's a nice boy, maybe a
little too full of uncritical enthusiasm

for his own good. It's a quality that's taken him down some peculiar alleys. He's not the brightest sparkler in the packet, but he listens well, and he's mentioned a few rather startling tidbits that may have rolled off the pillow, and that could be classified as Hot International Stuff. (It all has to do with that Mossadegh fellow you were writing about recently.) I have impressed upon Dear Davey that he is not to talk about these things with anybody but his Uncle George--excuse me, his Aunt Christine--but to tell me everything!

I will discreetly pass it all along to you, my darling newshound, when I see you in Paris next week.

Much love,
C.

Hotel de l'Odeon
Paris

Mr. Alden Carraway
c/o American Consulate
Kathmandu, Nepal

April 4

Dear Alden,

I have no idea whether this letter will find
you. If it does, it's a better man than I.
I'm writing this from Paris, where I came at
least in part to find you, and seem to have
missed you by a matter of days. The other
part of my visit, I guess, was to try to
find myself, as I suppose you're doing in
your monastery or ashram.

It's amazing the things you can see when you
step back a few paces. Some of the picture
is not very pretty. There are parts of it
that make me despair; other parts fill me
with an enormous patriotic pride. I have
always imagined myself a "good American";
but I think I'm only just beginning to
understand what that means.

I saw Chaplin's "Limelight" last night on
the Champs-Élysées with Jake Barnes, who's

taken me under his wing since I arrived in
Paris. He has wonderful things to say about
you, which makes me very proud. Anyway,
it was a marvelous movie. One of my first
official acts in Washington was to sign off
on a recommendation to Attorney General
Brownell that Chaplin's expulsion from the
United States not be reviewed. I thought it
made sense from that side of the Atlantic.
Now I wonder. America is a great country,
Alden, the greatest experiment in liberty
the world has ever seen. Whether an artist's
views are the same as mine or Dorothy
Kilgallen's or Joe McCarthy's, we ought
perhaps to have room for their expression.
In fact, I'm beginning to think we <u>must</u> make
that room, if we are to survive.

I'm so sorry to have missed you here
in Paris, Alden. I have your general
whereabouts from Jake. Don't blame him for
telling me where you are. There was and is
a lot I have to say to you about you and me
and the missed opportunities and the lost
years. I have a feeling you and I can bridge
those gaps, but we'll need to sit down
together for a few long afternoons. Please
write and let me know how you're doing. I am
longing to see you.

Your loving father

Jacob Barnes
Paris Herald Tribune
38, rue de Berri
Paris 16, France

April 5th, or thereabouts

Fowler,

Well, get your gin-soaked ass over here!
How the hell are you? How the hell have you
been? If you see any Americans in Saigon,
shoot them. With my permission. That's the
only goddam language they understand.
It'll be damn good to see you. Fuck Philby,
it's his loss. Bud Powell is playing at
Le Bar Negre--not that sort of watered-
down oompah music you Brits call jazz, but
something damn honest and true. The kind of
thing you need to hear, before you jump to
too many conclusions about America.

I'll introduce you to my new pal Nick
Carraway. You may remember--I sent you his
novel years ago, the one about the gangster
who falls in love with the rich dame. Since
he's been here he's been coming in for a
good dose of your damn old-Europe Yank-
bashing, which is doing him some good. The
Europeans are sore as hell over Chaplin, and
I think a few scales are beginning to drop
from Carraway's eyes. He still has too many

illusions about America, and we can't cure what's wrong with America with illusions. Damn fine writer though, and a good man, though he can't always hold his liquor.

Don't try to get him to any of your favorite bordels, although he could use it. He's tied up like a knot below the belt. Anyway, he's got this idea his wee-wee is too small. Told me the other night when he was tight. Tells everybody when he's tight, I hear. He'll tell you if you get him tight.

Just as glad Philby won't be here. I don't want to get in the middle of that. Spender doesn't trust him worth a damn, but he's been sucking up to Kristol like nobody's business, and they've gotten to be thick as thieves.

Anyway, we'll have entertainment. McCarthy's Two Stooges, Cohn and Schine, hit town tonight, fresh from a boffo engagement in Frankfurt. You must have read a word or two about it, even out there in the fucking Orient. So come!

Yr. loyal partner in depravity,

Barnes

Apartment C
14½ MacDougal Street
New York

April 5, 1953

Dear Mr. Carraway,

That sounds so formal, now that we've been
writing each other back and forth like
this, and you're not married anymore.
(Oh, goodness--I don't know what I meant
by that!) I remember a lot of the people
on the show used to call you Nick, and I
always called you Mr. Carraway, and one
of the Snicklekids--do you remember Mary
Richards?--used to tease me about it. She
said when she grew up, she wasn't going to
let anyone push her around, and she would
always call her boss by his first name.
Anyway, I hope I'm not sounding too much
like a small-town girl from the Midwest. I'm
trying to be a real New Yorker now. I wear
black leotards and peasant blouses and eye
makeup, just like all the other kids who
come out to Washington Square Park on Sunday
to sing folk music. This week a few people
even recognized me. Some of them even took
my picture--a couple of men in suits and
snap-brim hats and dark glasses--I guess
they were tourists, they didn't look like
the Greenwich Village types.

But you really are my best friend, you know.
Whenever something important happens to me,
or I find myself really thinking deeply
about something (not that I'm saying my
thoughts are so terribly deep or anything),
I always wish you were here. New York can
be a lonely town, and I sometimes think
how good it would be to have a shoulder to
cry on, and someone to say, there, there,
Ronnie, you're going to be all right.

Oh, I know I'm being silly. I hope you won't
think I'm just a silly girl and stop writing
to me altogether.

Your friend always,

Ronnie

Hotel George V

31 Avenue George V
Paris 8eme
France

Roy Cohn
Suite 7A

April 7

Dear Uncle Robert,

Thanks for your note of encouragement.
That's right, you lived in Paris for a few
years in your reckless youth, didn't you?
When you were writing your pinko novels.
Don't worry, your books are safe!

Davey and I have been having a ball on this
trip. You wouldn't believe the European
press. They're really spazzing out over us,
but they're dumb enough to jerk around--it's
like throwing a bone for a dumb dog and you
throw it over the fence and the dog smashes
into the fence chasing it. Really funny!
Davey wrote a poem I think you'll like. Here
it is:

    Europe is a fucking whore
    Parlay-voo francais
    Why we saved 'em in the war

Is more than I can say
The Frenchies kissed our G.I. ass
Voulay-voo Paree
Now they give us frogs and gas,
The men are slow, the girls are fast,
Well I for one will take a pass
Who gives a fart? Not me!

Is this a talented kid or what? I made him
sign it and then I grabbed it and posted it
at the concierge's desk. Davey went bananas!
He chased me through the lobby of the
Georges V trying to swat me with a rolled-up
magazine! I was yelling "Commie swine" and
ducking for cover. It was a hoot! The snooty
hotel manager tried to put a damper on us,
but I dropped Senator McCarthy's name and he
left us alone. What a dork!

Speaking of people who seem to think a lot
of themselves, your pal Barnes showed up
at the press conference we had the day we
got here. You're right, he's an arrogant
sonofabitch. He asked what kind of books
we were trying to weed out of the USIA
libraries. I said, "What kind of books do
you think, Mr. Barnes?" He said, "If I were
fighting communism, I don't think I'd give
people any books at all." I'm not sure what
he meant by that, but I'm going to pass his
name along to our staff.

I can see why you liked Paris. There's something going on every minute here--no bull!!!! Maurice is taking us to a nightclub tonight--a "boat," they call them here. I'll keep you posted when I can grab a moment to write. We'll be here a few more days, and then heading home to file a report for the Senator.

Love to Aunt Frances.

Roy

Submission to the <u>Herald Tribune</u>
Music Review
Francis Paudras

April 7, 1953

Attn: M. Barnes

PARIS--The great American pianist Bud Powell
played what turned out to be two solo
sets at Le Bar Negre last night. Hampered
at first by a sluggish rhythm section of
Parisian locals, M. Powell soon left them
behind. First the drummer, then the bass
player trailed off, and stood watching M.
Powell in disbelief. They did not return to
the bandstand for the second set.

Powell took familiar standards like "Tea
for Two" and newer bebop compositions like
"Ornithology," and led them through a series
of runs up and down the keyboard, in and
out of time and melody, crashing up against
chords that seemed to have positioned
themselves at unexpected junctions around
hairpin turns, then emerging unscathed on
the other side, but for a few distinguishing
wisps plucked from the chord, much like
other American geniuses such as les Keystone
Cops or Messrs. Abbott and Costello driving
their flivvers into a barn and coming
out the other side. There is no hayseed
on M. Powell, but he exhibits the same
consummate skill and timing masked as utter
recklessness.

On the night this reporter ventured out
to review M. Powell's performance, the
audience included Messrs. Roy Cohn and G.
David Schine, the associates of the American
Senator Joseph McCarthy, at a table with
the Vichy collaborator Maurice Chevalier.
They left during the first set, as M. Powell
was negotiating a breathtaking passage of
"You Brought a New Kind of Love to Me."
At another table, nearer the bandstand,
was a group that included M. Jacob Barnes,
managing editor of the Paris Herald Tribune,
M. Thomas Fowler, Asian correspondent of
the Times of London, M. Nicholas Carraway,
an American novelist, and Mlle. Christine
Jorgensen, best known for her recent medical
procedure in Copenhagen.

At the end of the second set, M. Powell
joined this latter group, and it was then
that the evening took a bizarre and very
nearly a tragic turn. After a round of
drinks, M. Powell's behavior began to change.
He seemed to take offense at a remark by M.
Carraway. Then, without warning, he leaped
up from his chair, grabbed the bottle, and
smashed it against the table, cutting his
hand in the process. The white tablecloth
was quickly drenched in blood.

M. Barnes took M. Powell by the arm and
calmed him, guiding him to the next table
where he deftly removed the sliver of
glass from M. Powell's hand. All this

time he was speaking quietly, revealing a surprising knowledge of the Harlem of M. Powell's boyhood. The great musician visibly relaxed as they discussed shops and street corners and small nightclubs, and musicians like Willie "The Lion" Smith and James P. Johnson. Their conversation turned to Kansas City, where M. Barnes was raised. M. Powell's eyes lit up. "Did you know Lester Young and Count Basie?" he asked. "Did you hear Bird play back in KC?"

"I left Kansas City before the war," M. Barnes answered. "Before the great jazz clubs opened. But I did hear Scott Joplin play in Sedalia, when I was a kid. His music had dignity and truth, the truth from which all music must start. Your playing has that truth, too. I visited New York a number of times in the Thirties. But then the war started, and I did not leave Europe in those years. I heard stories, though, about the after-hours sessions at Minton's Playhouse, and the greatness of Thelonious Monk."

M. Powell's eyes grew dim, and he seemed to be somewhere else. "Minton's," he said. "I was there, you know, the night they raided the place. They went after Monk. They came after him with clubs, and they put the cuffs on him."

"I heard about that," M. Barnes said. "You wouldn't let the cops take him. You told them, 'You don't know what you're doing. You're mistreating the greatest musician in the world!'"

"That's what they say," M. Powell said. "I don't remember nothing."

"They hit you," M. Barnes said. "They clubbed you on the head with a nightstick."

"Me," M. Powell said proudly. "Not Monk. Me. I stopped them from hitting Monk. I know, because when I woke up, we were in a cell together, and Monk was all right. They arrested the greatest musician in the world, but they didn't hit him. Me. Not Monk."

There are rumors that M. Powell suffers from nervous disorders, as a result of that blow. It is apparent, however, that his mistreatment at the hands of the iniquitous American justice system has not affected his genius.

--Francis Paudras

Paudras - stick to the music, and cut out all the other crap. What is this, a music review or a soap opera? If it's a news story, you buried the lead.   — Barnes

Hotel de l'Odeon
Paris

April 7, 1953

Dear Ronnie,

I'm afraid that I have a lot to learn about
life, and am just beginning to find out how
much. Earlier tonight Barnes took me out to
a bistro to hear some jazz. At least Barnes
said it was going to be jazz, but it's a far
cry from what my generation danced to, in
those halcyon days we called the Jazz Age.
Afterward, the pianist--an American Negro
named Powell--came over to our table, and
I managed to insult him. I was trying to
be friendly, and I said, "Is that what
you hepcats nowadays call beep-bop? Like
that Thelonious Monkey and all those other
strange musicians who wear those outlandish
sunglasses and goatees?" I realized even as
I was saying it that I was making a total
ass of myself and trying to pretend to know
something I know nothing about, but I wasn't
prepared for what followed.

He came at me, with intent to kill. He
smashed a bottle and brandished it in my
face, his hand bloody from the flying glass.
It was truly frightening. But Barnes stepped
in between us, and I don't know how he did

it, but without raising his voice or using any physical force, he gently steered Mr. Powell away. He sat him down at a nearby table, and talked to him for maybe half an hour. Ronnie, he was marvelous!

After that, Mr. Powell and I shook hands and made up. I apologized, and he patted my shoulder and said, "I get crazy sometimes, man." We walked him back to his hotel, to see that he arrived safely--and to make sure that he didn't drink any more--and I found myself looking at his eyes, deeply troubled and profoundly calm at the same time, and wishing I could talk to him the way Barnes can. My experiences are starting to seem awfully shallow to me. There's tragedy in that Negro's eyes, and I suspect that behind every tragedy there's a hero.

Your devoted friend,

Nick

Hotel Danemark

21, Rue Vavin

Paris 6e, France

April 8

Dear Helen,

An added surprise on my Paris trip. You'll
have read about the notorious Christine
Jorgensen--the American soldier who recently
went from a him to a her? It turns out she's
a close pal of Barnes's, and she joined us
on our Paris pub crawl (incognito, to evade
my journalistic brethren--or perhaps they
stayed away out of deference to Barnes). She
turns out to be a very attractive woman--the
photographs don't do her justice. And quite
feminine ... no, womanly might be a better
word. She has a maturity about her that one
does not always encounter in one so young,
and rarely if ever in Americans.

Speaking of which, Barnes is top drawer.
Hard to believe he's a Yank. I saw him
defuse a situation between an American
writer named Carraway and a nigger piano
player last night. I would have simply tried
to get us all out of there, but Barnes sat
down and talked to the fellow. Had him
telling us his life story. Carraway, Miss

Jorgensen and I listened spellbound. The four of us ended the evening by seeing the nigger chap home to a small flat in the 5th.

Not sure what to make of this Carraway-- mostly, I believe, because he's not sure what to make of himself. I believe he's someone who has always lived through others. Perhaps that's what made him such a good novelist, although he's only written one book. Barnes sent it to me years ago--I believe he's sent it to everyone he knows --and I understood why he liked it, but I'm afraid it was too American for me. At any rate, Barnes has quite taken him under his wing.

Perhaps one had to have lived through what Barnes and Carraway and his man Gatsby lived through in their war. Barnes is fond of saying "one of us," a phrase which he tinges, however, with irony. He includes me when he says it, for better or for worse, but I don't belong. There's something that always set that generation apart. Certainly my crowd at Oxford thought so. We never got over being the generation that didn't go to war. Which meant, of course, that we also were not the generation that didn't come back. And that often seemed to be the hardest part. Barnes represents something to us, and that may be part of the reason he is held in such high regard. That, and

of course the fact that he's a damned good
journalist and a damned good drinker.

Spender and Auden and Isherwood, when they
weren't talking about revolution, were
talking about the coming war. They started
anticipating it by about 1922, I'd say. I
suppose anything was better than looking
back at the classes just before us at
Oxford, which essentially didn't exist. It
was eerie.

Well, the coming war came, did it not? And
I can't say we're the better for it. I
don't know that I like being "one of us."
I'm tired of having to choose up sides,
and I suspect many of my friends feel the
same way. "Taking sides" these days means
either being for or against America, and
both positions grow more and more untenable.
Still, it must be very strange for those
veterans of what they used to call The Great
War, to suddenly no longer be numbered among
the happy few.

Now, about that divorce ...

Sincerely yours,

Thomas

9 April

Dear Jake,

Thanks for the evening. Paris was wonderful.

How have you stayed away from America for so long? Were you trying to prove something? To yourself? Because you're American to the core, darling, and you love the damn country. Always have, always will. I know, because I don't.

I don't hate America. It's like my male equipment. Painful to admit, even to myself, that I didn't need it, because everyone said it was the greatest thing in the world. But easy to shed, once I'd made up my mind. I don't hate men (at all), but I hated myself, being a man, and I'm still learning to separate myself from that self-hatred. But the physical parts themselves ... it's strange but true. They're gone and forgotten. No nostalgic backward glances, no regrets.

So I know what it's like to leave something and not miss it. And if that was how you were when you talked about America, I'd recognize it in you. But you're not like that. Something else is inside you.

And I like it, you old bear.

Love,
C

Dr. Christian Hamburger
Director of Special Surgery
Royal Hospital
Copenhagen, Denmark

April 9, 1953

Dear Mr. Barnes,

Miss Christine Jorgensen has related to me
your correspondence with her regarding your
condition.

Without a physical examination, of course,
it would be impossible for me to venture
an informed evaluation of your candidacy
for the kind of procedure we can offer
here. However, I must say that on the basis
of Miss Jorgensen's descriptions, I am
intrigued by the possibilities. Medical
science has made enormous strides in the
decades since you suffered your disability,
and I flatter myself that here at the clinic
we have been at the forefront--dare I say
the cutting edge?--of the technology from
which you might hope to benefit.

Copenhagen is a day's journey from Paris.
While it would be unprofessional of me to
dangle expectations, I am optimistic enough
to encourage you to make the trip.

Very Truly Yours,

Dr. Christian Hamburger
Director of Special Surgery

(ENCRYPTED AND DECODED)
(4/9)
FROM: ALLEN DULLES
TO: IRVING KRISTOL

CAN'T ALLOW STRONG FIGURE LIKE DEGAULLE
TO CONSOLIDATE POWER IN FRANCE. OPERATION
DESERT RAT READY TO ROLL, AND THAT'S OUR
OUT-OF-TOWN TRYOUT, THE NEW HAVEN OF OUR
STRATEGY. IF IT'S A HIT, OPERATION ELBA OUR
BROADWAY OPENING. DOMINO THEORY. IF IT PLAYS
IN IRAN, NO REASON IT WON'T WORK IN FRANCE.
OPERATION ELBA SWINGS INTO GEAR. EUROPE
ROLLS OVER LIKE CIRCUS POODLE. NEED TO KEEP
FRANCE WEAK AND CONFUSED.
DULLES

(ENCRYPTED AND DECODED)
(4/9)
FROM: ALLEN DULLES
TO: ROBERT COHN

DO YOU REALLY HAVE THAT NEPHEW OF YOURS
UNDER CONTROL? HAVE DOUBTS ABOUT THE WISDOM
OF THIS STRATEGY.

DULLES

(ENCRYPTED AND DECODED)
(4/9)
FROM: IRVING KRISTOL
TO: ALLEN DULLES

I HAVE A PLAN FOR FRANCE. WE'RE BUILDING
UP ONE OF THEIR POLITICIAN-OF-THE-MONTH-
CLUB CIPHERS, PIERRE MENDES-FRANCE, TO GIVE
THE ILLUSION HE'S A FIGURE OF STRENGTH. BUT
WE'RE SECRETLY INDOCTRINATING HIM TO BELIEVE
THAT WINE IS SAPPING THE FRENCH MORAL FIBER.
WHEN THE MOMENT IS RIGHT, WE'LL HAVE HIM
PHOTOGRAPHED DRINKING MILK--THEN THE WHOLE
GOVERNMENT SHOULD COLLAPSE AGAIN.

KRISTOL

(ENCRYPTED AND DECODED)
(4/9)
FROM: ALLEN DULLES
TO: IRVING KRISTOL

BRILLIANT. YOU'VE GOT A FUTURE AS A
TROUBLEMAKER, KRISTOL. NOW ABOUT THE COHN-
SCHINE JUNKET. NOT COMFORTABLE WITH LEAVING
THIS IN CARRAWAY'S HANDS.

DULLES

(ENCRYPTED AND DECODED)
(4/9)
FROM: ROBERT COHN
TO: ALLEN DULLES

I HAVE A PLAN FOR ROY. OF COURSE THAT FAGGOT
NEPHEW OF MINE WILL FUCK THINGS UP. WE TURN
IT TO OUR ADVANTAGE. YOU NEED TO BE MORE
CREATIVE IN YOUR THINKING, DULLES. SEMPER
PARATUS. REMIND ME SOME TIME TO TELL YOU
ABOUT MY THEORY OF USING DIFFERENT SIDES OF
YOUR BRAIN.

COHN

(ENCRYPTED AND DECODED)
(4/9)
FROM: ALLEN DULLES
TO: ROBERT COHN

THIS IS A GOVERNMENT SERVICE. PLEASE WATCH
YOUR LANGUAGE. DO NOTHING WITHOUT CLEARING
WITH ME.

DULLES

(ENCRYPTED AND DECODED)
(4/9)
FROM: IRVING KRISTOL
TO: ALLEN DULLES

YOU KNOW HOW ROBERT COHN IS. IF HE ENTERS
THE PICTURE, WE NEED TO THROW ALL OUR PLANS
OUT THE WINDOW. BUT WE'VE IMPROVISED BEFORE,
WE CAN DO IT AGAIN. MEANWHILE, IF WE WANT TO
INCLUDE BARNES IN THE PICTURE, WE NEED TO
BRING HIM INTO FOCUS SOON. THE COHNS APPEAR
TO HAVE A GRUDGE AGAINST HIM. BARNES AND
CARRAWAY HAVE BECOME THICK. I'D SAY IT'S
TIME TO MOVE THE CARRAWAY PAWN FORWARD, OPEN
UP THAT GAMBIT. OF COURSE, THIS COULD MEAN
THROWING YOUR MAN TO THE WOLVES, IF WE GO TO
IMPROVISATION MODE. PROBLEMS WITH THAT?

KRISTOL

(ENCRYPTED AND DECODED)
(4/9)
FROM: ALLEN DULLES
TO: IRVING KRISTOL

DON'T WASTE WORDS. THESE CABLES COME FROM
OUR BUDGET. CAN THROW CARRAWAY TO WOLVES IF
NEED BE. BARNES TOO?

DULLES

(ENCRYPTED AND DECODED)
(4/9)
FROM: ROBERT COHN
TO: ALLEN DULLES

ALLIE--DON'T WORRY ABOUT A THING. TRUST ME.

ROBBIE

(ENCRYPTED AND DECODED)
(4/9)
FROM: IRVING KRISTOL
TO: ALLEN DULLES

I'M AN INTELLECTUAL, REMEMBER? TO ME, THIS
IS BEING CONCISE. NO PROBLEM IN THROWING
BARNES TO THE WOLVES. IF WE CAN USE HIM,
ALL TO THE GOOD. BUT I'VE BEEN TALKING TO
PHILBY, AND HE TELLS ME THERE'S SCUTTLEBUTT
OVER IN MI-6 ABOUT ENCOUNTER HAVING TIES TO
THE COMPANY. I'M THINKING IF COHN ENDS UP
MAKING BARNES THE SCAPEGOAT, WE CAN DISTRACT
ATTENTION AWAY FROM CERTAIN OTHER ENCOUNTER
EDITORS, SUCH AS YOUR HUMBLE SERVANT.

KRISTOL

April 9, 1953

Dear ... Nick ... ?

There, I said it. Do I seem like a forward,
brassy girl? I hope not. It sounds strange
... but nice.

I guess you did make a mistake with Mr.
Powell about Mr. Monk, but how could you
know? I wouldn't have, either, just a few
days ago.

The thing about Mr. Monk is, he's a genius
and he's been so terribly mistreated that
his friends feel really protective of him.
I found that out when a couple of Mr.
Sheinbloom's friends (a very gentlemanly
Turkish man named Ahmet Ertegun, and his
partner, a real Noo Yawker named Jerry
Wexler) took me to a club in Greenwich
Village where they said Thelonious Monk
would be playing. It was a secret, because
they couldn't advertise it, because Monk--
that's what they call him, Monk--do I sound
like a sophisticated New Yorker?--isn't
allowed to play in any clubs in New York.
Mr. Wexler told me why. It's because jazz is

a blow for freedom, and The Establishment
wants to wipe out freedom. So Monk was
arrested on some trumped-up charge, and now
he can't get a cabaret card, which means
now he can't play his music anywhere in New
York, and that's about the most unfair thing
I ever heard, next to what happened to you.

Anyway, the musicians were already playing
when we got there, and suddenly there was a
hush over the whole room, and I looked up,
and the kitchen door opened, and out walked
Monk. He has an aura about him that makes
you tingle. He started playing, and at first
nothing seemed to fit. All these notes--they
weren't exactly chords, they were more like
jammed together as if he was squeezing them
into a ball in his fist instead of playing
them. But then I started to hear them
differently, and suddenly bit by bit they
started to come together, as if these were
the harmonies of the angels from the heaven
of whatever strange world it was that Monk
lives in, and all I could think was, "I wish
I could sing that." Sometimes I get so tired
of "Michael, Row the Boat Ashore."

Then somebody yelled out "Cops!" and the
next thing I knew, they were hurrying Monk
off the bandstand and out the kitchen door
again, and suddenly four policemen came
running in, swinging nightsticks. It was
scary! They wouldn't let any of us leave

until they'd taken everyone's name and
address down.

So I guess that's why Mr. Powell acted so
odd. I know it didn't really have anything
to do with you. It's Monk--people get fierce
about him. You should have seen how they
took care of him that night with the police.
I never saw anything like it.

Funny, I always thought of policemen as our
friends. But then, I always thought of our
government as good people, protecting us
from the Communists. But so many things are
happening to me. In many ways, I'm not the
girl you knew. I hope you'd still like me. I
hope you'd like me better. I feel like I'm
not a girl anymore, I'm a woman.

Your special friend,

Ronnie

April 9, 1953

Dear Jackie,

Hi, girl--surprised to hear from me? How
are things at the Martha Washington? Still
breaking all the rules--and getting away
with it??? Ha ha.

I need you to tell me something ... I hope I
haven't made a terrible mistake. I really,
really, really hope, because I wrote the
letter a few days ago, and I already sent it
off, and then I started thinking about ...
well ... if there's a guy you think maybe
you really like more than anyone else in the
world, and he's a long way away, like maybe
Paris, France, and you wrote him a letter,
and in it you said, "I'm not a girl anymore
... I'm a woman," would he get the wrong
idea?

Can you keep a secret? I went to this party
with Mr. Sheinbloom at his friend Jerry
Wexler's, who owns a record company. The
Weavers were there (except Mr. Seeger), and
Burl Ives, and we were going to hear this
wonderful new blind singer and piano player
that Mr. Wexler's label has just signed.

He was "real" cool! And you know what? He sang this one song where he needed some girl singers in the background, and Jerry told me to get up with these two Negro girls named Ruth and Lavern. I think they were the best singers I ever heard, and I had no business singing with them, but they were awful nice to me, and told me to keep at it.

Afterward this young guy named Chuck came up to me. He's a singer and a songwriter from St. Louis, he's here trying to get a recording contract, and he told me he really liked the way I sang, and the way I looked. He couldn't get over my eye makeup, and I told him it was just Maybelline, that all the girls down in Greenwich Village wear lots of eye makeup, to look more sophisticated. I told him back in my school days in Winnetka, I thought the height of being grownup was to wear tight dresses and lipstick, and high-heeled shoes, but that all seemed so teenage now.

Anyway, the way he kept looking at me when we were talking, it made my skin go all goose-bumpy, and I could tell he wanted to, you know ...

But just then there was a big commotion and Mr. Sheinbloom had gone all purple and couldn't breathe, and he was saying "The cat! The cat!" Mr. Wexler's cat had gotten

out of the bedroom and jumped in his lap
and Mr. Sheinbloom is deathly allergic, and
I had to take him home, so I didn't get to
see Chuck again. But that other guy from the
Weavers, whose name I can never remember,
drove us, and after we got Mr. Sheinbloom to
bed he insisted on driving me home.

And I don't know, Jackie, maybe it was that
I was still so hot and bothered or whatever
from being with Chuck, but next thing I knew
... well ... you know that thing I was, that
I didn't want to be? Well I'm not anymore.

The worst of it is, I still can't think of
his name! They say a girl never forgets her
first. I guess I'll never remember.

Your friend,

Ronnie

PS. Do you think it was OK? The letter, I
mean?

Robert Cohn Associates
1853 M Street NW, Suite 830
Washington, DC

April 10

Dear Roy,

I had breakfast up on the hill with your
boss this morning. McCarthy is as proud
of you as if you were his nephew. Believe
me, he's following the headlines from your
trip like they were box scores from the
Washington Senators.

Over coffee, he looked a little down, and
for a moment I thought I sensed a little
disappointment that there hadn't been
anything really climactic. "A capper," he
said, dabbing distractedly at a spot of
egg yolk on his tie. "There's gotta be a
capper!"

But then he looked up at me, and a big
grin spread across his face. "He'll do
it," he said. "The kid's got imagination.
The kid's got balls! You watch, Cohn--that
nephew of yours'll come up with something
spectacular!"

I tell you, Roy, watching that smile spread
across that five o'clock shadow (this is

morning, mind you) it was like watching
the sun break through storm clouds over a
Wisconsin swamp. That man thinks a lot of
you. He's expecting something big.

I know you won't let him down.

Your proud uncle,

Robert

April 10, 1953

Ronnie,

Don't worry, kiddo. Men are all alike. If a
man likes you that way, he <u>suspects</u> you with
every man who ever lived, but he doesn't
really <u>think</u> you'd ever do it with anyone
except him. So don't worry, it never hurts
to keep 'em guessing.

So ... little Ronnnnieeeeee!!!!!!!!! Woo
woo!!!! But here's a word of advice from a
babe who's fallen off a few cabbage trucks
in her day. You can have a fling or two, but
when you get ready for the One That Counts,
here are your Aunt Jackie's Three Rules for
Choosing a Man.

Rule Number One: Think Older.

Rule Number Two: Think Jewish.

So far, your friend Wexler sounds he's got
potential, but don't ever forget Rule Number
Three:

Think Broadway.

All that jazzy-jazz and folky-folk stuff
will never get you anywhere. This is New
York, kiddo.

Love and kisses,

Jackie

FROM THE DESK OF:
ALLEN DULLES

By Diplomatic Pouch
April 10, 1953

Carraway,

Sorry to have had to leave you out in the
cold through all this. I trust in your heart
of hearts you never doubted that I, and the
Agency, were behind you, but for obvious
reasons it was important that this situation
be allowed to unfold in a way that would
arouse no suspicion whatsoever.

Mind you, the McCarthy development was not
one that we put into play, but here at the
Company I've encouraged a tradition of seat-
of-the-pants adapting to circumstances that
I learned from my mentor, Wild Bill Donovan.
So when the junior senator gave us a way
to position you deep under cover where you
could do the most good, it was a gift we
had to seize. I apologize if it caused any
difficulties for you personally. You can't
make sausage without letting a little blood.

I've kept a close eye on you. Believe me
when I say we were never going to let
anything bad happen to you. There were
moments when we were on the verge of

stepping in, but instead we watched with
gratified fascination as your instincts took
you in exactly the right direction. You're
good, Carraway. You're damned good. Someday,
when this is all over and the world is safe,
you and I need to sit down with a bottle of
bourbon and talk about what you knew, and
how you managed it.

The pieces are moving into place. The time
is now.

Bring in Barnes.

Dulles

Lady Brett Ashley

Grand Hotel
New Delhi

April 10

Dear Jake,

   Bulletin from the spirit world: the spirit was willing, but the flesh was stronger. It seems you can't teach an old cat new tricks.

   Not strictly true, darling. The Maharishi taught me a trick or two I would never have dreamed possible. A nifty little number called tantric sex. Orgasms composed of two parts butterfly wing and five parts diesel locomotive. And I'm not talking about the Brighton local, darling, I'm talking about the Orient Express.

   Oh, I know you hate it when I tell you these things. But you love it, too. Given our rotten damned circumstances, it's the closest we've got to intimacy, isn't it? And you've always been the only one I could talk to. Even five thousand miles away, you're still the man I want to run to whenever I've been naughty. Because no matter whom

I've been naughty with, Jake darling, it's really always you. Like that shah from the Middle East I was seeing just before I left Paris. Always told him I was in love with you. True, too.

I've left the ashram. The Maharishi was sweet, he begged me to stay, but you know, I'm just not much of a one-guru gal. And truth be told, darling, at my age you don't want to lie still too long. It's harder to spot the wrinkles on a moving target. The Maharishi is surrounded by all those guileless, willing twenty-three-year-old heiresses with firm titties and legs like baguettes. He was sweet, he offered to send them all away if I'd only stay another week, but you don't live a half a century as a temptress without picking up a few practical bits of wisdom.

So I'm down, but not out. Down from the mountaintop, that is. I'm in New Delhi, making up my mind which way to let the wind blow me next. I'd love to come back to Paris. I miss you, you know? But it's not going to happen right away.

I met a young chap at the monastery. Alden. Young and vigorous and very American, and I guess he reminds me of you--or what you would have been,

darling, if it hadn't been for rotten
luck and that damned war. Remember
Pedro Romero, the bullfighter? Sort
of like that, only very American, and
of course I never let Alden see me
in good light. Not that there's any
good light at the monastery. I suspect
he'll be leaving there soon. I'm afraid
it turned out that the celibate life
wasn't for him, either. I'm afraid he's
quite smitten with me.

So I'll play this one out a little
farther, till my whiskers tell me
the magic's wearing thin, and then
I'll jump off the roof before I get
pushed. One of these days you'll hear
me scratching at your door again, with
a tale or two to tell. Have a bowl of
warm milk standing by.

Oh Jake, we could have had such a
damned good time together!

Love Always,

Brett

Atlantic Records
Interoffice Memo

Date: April 10

From: Wexler
To: A. Ertegun

Ahmet--

Let's keep an eye on this girl. She has nice
tits, which is reason enough, but there's
more. You heard her the other night singing
backup for Ray, which is in a way easy,
because Ray's doing shit no one ever did
before, so there's no right or wrong way
to do it, which is something you wouldn't
necessarily think about, because the other
half of it is so obvious--it's difficult as
all fuck, because no one ever did it before.

But the kid got up there with Ruthie and
LaVern, and hung in there. She mostly hit
all the right notes, which is too bad. But
every now and then she took a chance, and
once--maybe twice--she found something.

Right now she's singing that hootenanny
shit, and I don't want to push her too
hard into changing. She needs some time to
develop. She's spent too much fucking time
singing nursery rhymes to kiddies, and you

can tell. She's got an innocence about her that I hope she never loses completely, but she'll grow up fast enough in New York. Especially if she spends much time with guys like that kid-shtupper Sheinbloom.

She's learning the ropes, but she's not doing anything that challenges her musically, and pretty soon she's going to realize that. I think she could be another fucking Chris Connor.

What did you think of the Berry kid? I say pass on him. He's got his own style, and it ain't never gonna be our style. That hillbilly stuff may play in the Midwest. But this is fucking New York.

Jerry

Maurice Chevalier
_____

April 10

Mon cher Cohn,
I have been entertaining your nephew and his
friend (particularly the friend) according
to your instructions. Enclosed you will find
an account of expenses. Ca coute cher, mon
vieux. David aime bien le champagne.

Maurice

4/11/53

FROM: ROY COHN
HOTEL GEORGE V
PARIS

TO: ROBERT COHN
WASHINGTON DC

UNCLE ROBERT
TELL MCCARTHY AND DULLES DONT WORRY STOP
WORKING ON NEAT PLAN FOR CARRAWAY AND BARNES
STOP DAVEY SPENDING TOO MUCH TIME WITH
DEGENERATE FRENCH STOP CHEVALIER GOING TO
HIS HEAD STOP SICK OF EUROPE STOP NO BULL

ROY

FROM THE DESK OF:
ROBERT COHN

BY MESSENGER
April 11

Hey Allie,

Had a cable from Roy. He says he's working
on a "neat plan." I'll try to get details.
Knowing my idiot nephew it could be
entertaining, or it could be disastrous.
Very likely both. In any case, we should
be able to use it and still have complete
deniability. We want things unsettled in
France, right?

Robbie

FROM THE DESK OF:
ALLEN DULLES

By special courier

4/11

Cohn,

Don't let him do anything till I approve it.

Dulles

FROM THE DESK OF:
ROBERT COHN

BY MESSENGER

April 11

Allie-boy

Loosen up! Seat-of-the-pants, remember?

Robbie

Hotel de l'Odeon
Paris

April 11, 1953

Dear Ronnie,

I'm glad one of us is growing up. It
sometimes seems to me I've just grown old,
without managing any maturity at all.
I may have known more when I was young.
Back before you were even born, I actually
wrote a novel. It made a little splash at
the time, and then it went away. It was part
fiction, part memoir, about a man I knew, a
strange, friendless man named Gatsby, one
of nature's knaves and noblemen. He was my
neighbor one summer on Long Island, and then
he was murdered. He made such an impression
on me that I wrote a story about him, and
about some other people I knew.

Then I decided I was too grown up for such
silliness, and it was time that I entered
the real world. That was when I went into
advertising, and married Margery, and we had
Alden, and I decided I owed it to him to
be a good, responsible father. Which meant
working late every night, rarely seeing him,
ultimately sending him away to boarding
school in the East--the Millbrook School for
Boys, where he wrote me about being bullied
by an older boy named Bill Buckley. He

retaliated by telling everyone he was going to vote for Henry Wallace when he grew up, and in short order he was expelled from the school.

Would I have been a better father to Alden if I'd remained a starving novelist? I don't know. But now, I find myself looking back and wondering if I really wasted all those years, wondering if I had more books inside me waiting to come out. If I still have. Well, life has many mysteries.

You, Ronnie, are one of the sweeter of those mysteries. In your last few letters I've felt the change in you, and I realize that my old image of you as a naïve and innocent child no longer applies. Innocent, yes, and perhaps still trailing a few wisps of the naiveté I remember, but I can see that you're a woman now. Unfortunately for me, you are a very young woman, and I am fast on my way to becoming a very old man. Because you are the one person to whom I find my thoughts turning these days when life has me spinning like a dervish and staggering like a Bowery rum-pot. I hope you will take no offense when I say that if I were a younger man, Ronnie, and a better man, I would certainly find myself thinking of you in a way that my age and imperfections rule out of the question.

Your Friend,
Nick

4/12/53

FROM: MLLE CHRISTINE JORGENSEN
HOTEL D'ANGLETERRE
COPENHAGEN

TO: JAKE BARNES
PARIS HERALD TRIBUNE

JAKE DEAREST CALL ME STOP HOT PILLOW TALK
STOP LOVE CHRISTINE

Hotel de l'Odeon
Paris

April 12, 1953
By messenger to the <u>Paris Herald Tribune</u>

Jake--

Well, hallelujah and glory be! I've done it.
I've written that novel.

Well, okay, I haven't. But I've set pen to
paper with serious intent.

It feels good. It feels terrible. It feels
strange as bloody hell. I feel like a virgin
- "It hurts! Don't stop!" And it's all your
fault, you sonofabitch. I date this fall from
grace to the day you introduced me to Sartre
and De Beauvoir as "Carraway, the American
author." Now don't tell me I got it wrong,
and what you really said was "Carraway, the
other American."

Doctor, I've got this disease. I carry a
notebook around with me all the time and
scribble the most ridiculous goddamn shit.
I scrawl notes on menus and metro tickets.
Cryptic notes to myself that seem profound
as hell when I write them, and later on when
I excavate them from my pocket and read them
they look like the ravings of a hophead.

There's an idea. I'll become a reefer
addict. I'm halfway there anyway--I've
started smoking those things Sartre smokes.
I think they've made me shorter.

Jesus, Jake, I don't know another soul
in the world I could talk to about this.
Certainly not Sartre, who intimidates the
crap out of me as he pats my hand and
stares at me through those coke bottles he
wears. "We writers," he says, "we have a
responsibility to write." Like what he does
and what I'm trying to do could be described
by the same word. I've sat across a table
from Ike, and believe me, Sartre is a lot
more intimidating.

So far it's all just scraps and fragments.
Have sketched out a few plot lines, a few
novel ideas, but not sure any of them are
going anywhere. Here's a story I've been
thinking about: a guy, maybe a war vet,
living in the suburbs in the house with the
wife and the kids and the dog. He's doing
okay doing something he likes, but he wants
more. You know, more stuff, bigger house,
bigger car, bigger dog. So he takes an
executive job in a corporation, puts on a
gray flannel suit, and starts negotiating
the corporate ladder. Compromises, sells
out, drinks too much, learns valuable
lessons about self and society. Whaddya
think? I know, I can hear you saying it.

Crap.

Which is why I'm doing this by letter. If I
tried out something like that to your face
I'd get about as far as "a guy."

Wilson's back in town--Sloan Wilson, you
remember him? Nice young writer chap from
Connecticut or Casablanca or one of those
exotic places that starts with a 'C.' He
was with that young crowd at Jimmy Jones's
flat that night you got so tight you passed
out in the pissoir. Come to think of it,
you probably don't remember him. He's been
in Germany, heading back to Connecticut or
Casablanca. I'll run the idea past him over
steak frites at Balzar tonite. If he likes
it, I'll know it's shit.

God will sort it all out when He wakes up.
In the meantime, let's get together soon.
The booze doesn't taste right without you.

Your Devoted Friend,

Nick (of the Gillette Nicks)

Jake Barnes

April 12, 1953

by messenger

Nick my lad,

About fucking time, is all I can say. Stay
with it. Scraps and fragments are where it
all starts. Don't throw any of them out, at
least not yet. You never know where that
one true sentence that starts it all off is
going to come from, and sometimes you don't
recognize when you write it ... days or
weeks or months later, you'll open up an old
notebook, and then it's <u>Geez, I wrote that?
Don't even remember</u> ... <u>I must be a fucking
genius.</u>

But I don't think the chap in the gray
flannel suit is the way to go. It feels like
something you already wrote and rejected--
almost like <u>Trimalchio in West Egg</u> without
the Gatsby character. Like resurrecting the
other guy twenty years later, and who'd want
to read that?

And what else would you put into it? You'd
be writing out of memory, and out of anger.

You need a love-hate relationship with
your characters. You've got to take pure
sadistic delight in watching them get hit by
baseballs and trains and flying gash, but
you've got to love 'em at the same time. I
don't see you loving this fellow.

Get a little farther outside yourself. Find
a character you know, but don't understand.
And stay with it. Let's pass up the Deux
Magots this evening. Keep your ass in the
chair and write.

Conscience regards,

Ye Olde Jake

April 13, 1953

Brett darling,

I'm making my preparations to leave the ashram tomorrow. Darrell contacted me, from Teheran. He is sending someone here to brief me on what he wants me to do.

Darrell is such a strange man. I feel as though I can trust him completely, and then I'm not sure. It was he who made me see the vanity and superficiality of wanting to change the world. He made me realize that the world is within my own soul. Those of us who have achieved some measure of inner knowledge have a responsibility to use it to guide the destinies of the less enlightened.

At least I think that's right. Sometimes my mind feels so clouded I don't know what to believe any more. The only thing I'm sure of is the truth I found in your arms. You never had that kind of relationship with Darrell, did you? But no, of course you didn't. You're a little older than me, and you've had more experience in some ways, but I know I couldn't feel the way I do about you if you weren't pure in your heart.

Anyway, Darrell is sending this guy to see me, and he'll be here tonight. Actually, you know him — Lamont Cranston. I remember you telling me about Cranston and the secret wisdom he learned in the Orient. I hope he'll be able to help me unclear my mind. Darrell says Cranston has an important assignment for me. I'm glad. I'm ready to take on something meaningful.

love,
Alden

144

(ENCRYPTED AND DECODED)
(4/13)
FROM: NICHOLAS CARRAWAY
TO: ALLEN DULLES

THANKS FOR CONCERN AND REASSURANCE. LIFE IN
TATTERS, FRIENDS GONE, MARRIAGE OVER. WELL,
ILL WIND THAT BLOWS NO GOOD. WHAT DO YOU
MEAN, BRING BARNES IN? THOUGHT I WAS OUT
OF THIS. BARNES IS A FRIEND. HAD NOT BEEN
DEVELOPING HIM AS SOURCE, OR AGENT. WHY
DIDN'T YOU TELL ME SOONER? NOT SURE IT CAN
BE DONE NOW.

CARRAWAY

(ENCRYPTED AND DECODED) *(4/13)*
FROM: ALLEN DULLES
TO: NICHOLAS CARRAWAY

TELLING YOU NOW. STOP WHINING. BRING BARNES
IN. PLAN UNCHANGED. COORDINATE NEWSPAPERS,
STREET DEMONSTRATIONS, MILITARY UNREST,
GOVERNMENT INSECURITY IN PARIS. START
PLANTING STORIES.

DULLES

Paris
April 14, 1953

Dear Chris,

So, now that you're a woman, you can't keep
a secret?

I heard from your Dr. Hamburger. For once in
my life I don't know what the hell to say.
You know, I told you that night that you
were my first man, and you told me that it
didn't really count, because you weren't
really a man. At first I put it down to fag
talk, but it turned out that you were just
telling it straight.

I wasn't. There was one other time.

It was not long after the war. The first
war. Those years I didn't know what the hell
I was. Half man, half mad. I went after
gash like a fury. God knows why. I kept
taking girls to bed. And they'd laugh. Or
get angry. Or worst of all, be sensitive and
understanding.

I'd been playing tennis with this guy named
Robert. He wasn't one of us. That made it
easier. He was built like a tough guy--
he'd been a boxer in college. Middleweight
champion of Princeton. That didn't mean much
to me, but it meant a lot to Robert. Pretty,

looked a bit like Mel Ferrer. He told me it
was his first time, too, but he seemed to
know what he was doing. Then hated himself
when the lights were on.

It was just that one time. Hell, that was
enough to tell me it wasn't what I wanted,
though it felt good while it was happening.
Christ, anything feels good while it's
happening.

Robert wouldn't leave me alone after that.
Started hanging around with my friends.
Strutted and flexed his muscles a lot.
Invited himself along on trips. Made a play
for Brett. She went to bed with him a couple
of times. She told me. She always tells me.
She dropped him for the bullfighter and he
made a total ass of himself, and then we
didn't see him anymore.

And after that, nothing. Hell, nobody was
fucking anyway, in the Thirties. Everyone
getting married, or getting into politics,
or worrying about war. Brett would come up
sometimes and crawl in bed with me. Mostly,
she just wanted to be held. That's something
women think is swell, being held. Let me
know if it starts appealing to you, and then
I'll know you've really made the switch.

It was a damn good time to be a journalist
in Europe, You could still talk to the

crazies around Hitler, as long as you
weren't a kike--Christ, I am living in the
past, aren't I? After I spent a little time
with Goebbels and Speer and those bastards,
I stopped using words like that.

The War was something else. Everything was
raw, everything on the edge. Murrow told me
that when he was broadcasting up on those
rooftops--"This is London"--and the bombs
were crashing around him, there were women
literally crawling after him out on the
roofs.

But no more sex for me. Until that night I
met you. What did we do? Whatever it was, it
seemed to work. And whatever it was, I guess
we couldn't do it again the same way, could
we? And what are we to each other, now?
Friends? That doesn't seem to cover it. All
I know is, since that night, Brett doesn't
break my heart any more.

Fuck it. I can't live like this, and you
get the blame. Or the credit. I'm going to
Copenhagen.

Love,

Jake

4/14/53

FROM: LADY BRETT ASHLEY
GRAND HOTEL
NEW DELHI

TO: LARRY DARRELL
TEHERAN

DONT WORRY ABOUT KID STOP HES RIPE STOP ONE
SESSION WITH CRANSTON AND HES YOURS STOP
JUST ONE THING DARLING DONT EVER ASK ME TO
GO TO BED WITH CRANSTON AGAIN STOP HES TOO
KINKY EVEN FOR ME

BRETT

4/14/53

TO: REZA PAHLAVI
TEHERAN

REZA HONEY STOP SIT TIGHT STOP BY THIS TIME
NEXT WEEK WILL BE SITTING IN YOUR LAP ON
PEACOCK THRONE

LOVE BRETT

April 14, 1953

Dear Nick,

First of all, let me start out by saying that
I never thought of you as old. I've always
thought of you as my rock, though, from way
back when Snicklepoo and the Baby Sitter was
just starting--and wow, does that ever seem
like a long time ago!--a whole lifetime or
two. When things were going wrong on the set--
anything from cameras breaking down to worries
about the schedule to was I wearing the right
color dress, I always knew, and everyone
always knew, that you'd solve the problem. But
did you know that whenever you passed through
the set, all the girls--the makeup girl, the
head writer, everyone--would turn their heads
around just to watch you, and they'd giggle
and whisper, "He's so sexy."

And you know, I was so naïve back then, I'm
not sure I even knew what sexy was, exactly,
except maybe Eddie Fisher. So, you see, my
first definition of sexy was you! I guess you
think that's pretty silly, coming from a mere
girl. But it's true.

And you're not old.

Yours always,

Ronnie

Margery Pyle
40125 Oak Park Drive
Oak Park, Illinois

April 14, 1953

Nicholas,

I am back from Reno, and the divorce
is final. In the absence of any
compelling argument from your lawyer,
the judge granted all my property
settlement and alimony requests.

I am making a new life for myself.
I've met a fine man. His name is
William Fromme, he's an executive with
Welch's Grape Juice, and he's been
working with Mr. Welch to start a
new anti-Communist society that will
continue Senator McCarthy's fine work.
He has a little daughter, Lynette, and
he's raising her to be a real patriotic
American. We won't make the same
mistakes with her that we did--that you
did--with our son.

Anyway, I just want to tell you that
if I ever had any questions about your
manhood--and I did--and I know you did
--I just want to reassure you. You
don't measure up to a real man.

Margery

April 14, 1953

Dear Nick,

I found <u>Trimalchio in West Egg</u> at the Strand
Bookstore, and I read it through in one
sitting, and I loved it! It's everything
that I ~~love~~ like so much about you--
beautiful language, wise insights, and such
wonderful sympathy for how people can make
mistakes, and it only makes them more human.
I can just feel the love you have for all
your characters, even the awful ones, like
Tom. I wonder--was Jordan based on Mrs.
Carraway at all?

You're a wonderful writer! I just wish you
had written more novels. Well, it's not too
late. I believe there can be second acts in
all of our lives.

Ruth--Ruth Brown, her full name is--took
me to a recording session yesterday. I was
secretly hoping she'd ask me to sing backup
on it, but then I got there, and I listened
to the musicians Jerry had there, and the
backup singers, and I was praying they
wouldn't. Needless to say, they didn't.

She recorded four songs. I loved them all, but the one I liked best was called "Mama, He Treats Your Daughter Mean." Now, I can sing about mamas and daughters, but not like that. When Ruth sang it, you just knew she wasn't really calling her Mama for help. It's like, when she sings "Mama!" she's just telling the world she's got problems with a no-good man, but she's proud that she's woman enough to handle them. I wonder if I'll ever be woman enough to sing a song like that.

After the session, she took me up to a night club in Harlem called Smalls Paradise. There was a jazz quartet playing there, and they asked Ruth to get up and sing a number with them. She sang "Willow, Weep For Me," and it took my breath away. It's so different from the way she sings at the recording session. It seemed ... oh, here's where I realize I don't know anything about music, and I have so much to learn, but it seemed to me like it was different with the musicians. In the recording studio, singing the blues, she seemed to be listening to the rhythm section, and singing with them, but at Smalls Paradise she seemed to be listening to all the instruments, and almost becoming one of them.

I've never felt music like I felt it last night. I don't know if I could ever learn to do it, not the way Ruthie does. But there's something about New York that makes you feel like you can reinvent yourself, and everything is possible. I wish you were here.

Wishing,

Ronnie

PS. Jerry has given me records by Billie Holiday, Ella Fitzgerald, Dinah Washington, Chris Connor, and Anita O'Day, and I'm spending the day listening to them.

(ENCRYPTED AND DECODED)
(4/15)
FROM: IRVING KRISTOL
TO: LARRY DARRELL

HERE'S THE LATEST BATCH OF HEADLINE STORIES,
NEWS FEATURE ITEMS, AND EDITORIALS FOR THE
TEHERAN PRESS. WE'LL NEED A CHECKLIST ON OUR
PLANS. REMEMBER, THIS CAN'T GO WRONG. WE'LL
ONLY GET ONE CHANCE AT THAT CRYING COMMIE.

KRISTOL

(ENCRYPTED AND DECODED)
(4/15)
FROM: LARRY DARRELL
TO: IRVING KRISTOL

STORIES DISPATCHED TO THE LOCAL PRESS.
MILITARY SALTED WITH OUR MEN, READY FOR THE
COUP. GANG OF THUGS ROAMING THE STREETS
BREAKING WINDOWS, SHOUTING "DOWN WITH
MOSSADEGH!" NOW WE'VE UNLEASHED A SECOND
GANG OF BIGGER, UGLIER THUGS TO BEAT UP THE
FIRST GANG AND SHOUT "MOSSADEGH FOREVER!
COMMUNISM FOR IRAN!" SYMPATHY FOR THE ANTI-M
THUGS, CHAOS AND PANIC IN THE STREETS.

DARRELL

(ENCRYPTED AND DECODED)
(4/15)
FROM: IRVING KRISTOL
TO: LARRY DARRELL

IT HAD BETTER BE ENOUGH.
KRISTOL

(ENCRYPTED AND DECODED)
(4/15)
FROM: LARRY DARRELL
TO: IRVING KRISTOL

IRVING, YOU'RE TURNING INTO AN OLD WOMAN.

DARRELL

Hotel de l'Odeon
Paris

April 15, 1953
By messenger to the <u>Paris Herald Tribune</u>

Jake--

Notes, ideas, pieces. I don't remember
<u>Trimalchio</u> being this hard to lift off the
ground. It was hard to sustain, Lord knows,
although even then, huge chunks of it seemed
to write themselves, until I went back and
looked at them, and discovered that they
needed a whole lot more help from me before
they were ready to go out into the world.
But I never had any doubts about what I
wanted to write, or where it was heading.
Maybe it had to do with being young and
foolish. But mostly, I suspect, it was
because I really didn't know I was going to
be writing a novel. I just knew I had this
story that I had to lay out in front of me.
Now it's just the reverse. I know I want to
write something. I want to find characters
and let them loose on a story. I want to
hold a mirror up to the world. I want
to make a difference. I want to explore
corners of the human psyche, and I want to
unleash the power of words to illuminate the
darkness and find paths around corners and
discover uncharted islands where the natives
practice customs no one has ever heard of

before. I want words that will seduce women and turn grown men into boys again. I know that it matters.

And I don't have a story.

Ideas, by all means. Will-'o-the wisp ideas, prickles of current waiting to turn of a sudden to St. Elmo's fire and turn my typewriter into a blaze of light. And you're right, I don't want to turn a microscope on the flea circus of advertising. They can make you itch, but magnified to the hundredth degree, they're still just performing fleas.

So I'm looking for a character. I've been thinking about Alden ... he's the one I perhaps need most to understand. I wonder if I could write a novel from the point of view of a young man like him ... of a boy in the process of becoming a young man. I was thinking of the year that we sent Alden to an eastern prep school, which he left abruptly before the end of the semester, went into New York and wandered around, haunted by the sense that the world was full of phonies.

There's a character ... maybe not a character I know well enough. And is it enough of a story?
Or do I need a story at all? What if I

create the Nick that never was? Did you know
that after Jimmy Gatz died, and I went home
and moved back in with my parents and did
all that soul-searching that wound up being
<u>Trimalchio</u>, I almost said the hell with it
all? I was on the brink of just dropping
everything and hobo-ing it around the
country. I wonder if I could recreate that
alter ego. Maybe make him younger, change
the time frame ... a World War II vet,
chasing along on the road from one end of
the country to the other.

What do you think? Do I have anything yet?
Anything worth pursuing? I keep thinking
I'll know it when I hit it, but what if I
don't?

Spinning like a top,

Nick

Kempinksi Hotel
Berlin

April 16, 1953

Jake dear,

   You silly old bear. If you can't say it, I can.

   I love you.

   Even if it's the love that wouldn't even begin to know how to speak its name.

   Thank you for telling me more about yourself. I treasure it, I really do. I want to know all about you.

   I'll be traveling for a couple of speaking engagements, but I'll get back to see you as soon as I can. Dr. Hamburger is a dear. A big, brawny, outdoorsy Scandinavian type--you'd like him. And a sports fan. He says his ambition is to be the Stein Ericksen of sex surgery. A little jealous, dear? No need. He's too young for me. You know I prefer old grizzly bears like you.

   I don't understand war, and I suppose I never will. When I was thirteen and the war was just starting, I jumped up and down a lot and yelled about wanting to go over and kill Japs, but inside I knew I didn't really mean it.

   I've always been drawn to the intensity of experience, and I've always held back from it. Sex ... well, how could I open myself up completely when I didn't know who I was? I didn't want to make love to women, and I didn't want to make love to the kind of man who wanted to make love to a man.

I was too late for the war. I was drafted right after the armistice. I was relieved, and I was disappointed. I don't think I'm a physical coward, though I was always a sissy. I never minded being beaten up as a kid, as much as I minded that they wanted to do it. I wouldn't have been afraid of being hurt, or even of dying, as much as the possibility that I'd have to kill someone. I know you were a medical corpsman in the first war, and a journalist in the second, so you weren't directly involved in the business of killing people, except to the extent that everyone in a war is in that business. And you always knew that you might have to kill someone.

There was a sergeant in my basic training at Fort Dix. He'd been at Anzio, won the Silver Star with clusters. He was the toughest guy I'd ever met, and probably the bravest. And he had his secrets, and his torments. Including the one you're maybe thinking, but that was almost the least of it.

I sucked his cock, but what he really wanted was to suck mine. I tried to tell him I didn't do that, I didn't care about my cock, but I could see that it meant so much to him. But what he really needed came later, when I held him in my arms like a little boy, and he told me about the men--boys, really--he had killed. Described their faces to me. Every one of them. This tough, tough sergeant. I'd never heard him talk in anything except four-letter words. But he was almost poetic when he was describing their faces. And he remembered every one.

Men have it so hard. With all the heartache, I'm glad I am what I am.

Love, Christine

MOSSADEGH VICTORY ANNOUNCED

TEHERAN -- The Ministry of the Interior announced tonight that the Government had won the plebiscite on Premier Mohammed Mossadegh's appeal for authority to dissolve the Majlis (Parliament) by 2,043,389 votes to 1,207. The official announcement cleared the way for the President to dissolve the chamber, which he may do in a nationwide broadcast tomorrow.

(ENCRYPTED AND DECODED)
(4/16)
FROM: IRVING KRISTOL
TO: LARRY DARRELL

WHAT THE HELL? WE WERE SUPPOSED TO RIG THE MAJLIS TO THROW MOSSADEGH OUT! WHAT'S GOING WRONG?
KRISTOL

(ENCRYPTED AND DECODED)
(4/16)
FROM: LARRY DARRELL
TO: IRVING KRISTOL

DON'T WORRY. WE HAVE THE MILITARY.

DARRELL

By Messenger
April 16, 1953

Dear Nick--

What the hell, Nick, what the hell.

Writing doesn't have to be like that. Jesus,
we'd all shoot ourselves. You're a good
man, but you work too hard. Just remember
what I keep telling you--find that one
true sentence, write it down, and the rest
followeth like a pack of mangy dogs after a
bitch in heat.

As for seducing grown women and turning boys
into men, these are adventures that can
exist outside the written page. It can all
be fuckingly complicated, but maybe worth
the while.

Meanwhile, here's your chance to get your
feet wet again. After I finish tomorrow's
column, I'm heading up to Denmark for a
couple of weeks. I'm going to ask you to
fill in for me for one of those weeks. I've
got that kid Buchwald from the copy desk set
for the other. I'll fill you in when I can.

Yours,
Jake

PS. Thanks for minding the store.

THE BARNES DOOR

PARIS--When I was ten years old, my old man took me to the Tercentenary Exposition in Jamestown, Virginia. I ate Jell-O, and I saw moving pictures, and I watched a carriage move along a street without a horse attached to it. My father told me "Son, America is the greatest country in the world." I believed it then, and I believe it now.

The difference is that then I thought it was an eternal truth, as infinite as the air we breathe. Now I know it's something we have to work at to keep it that way. Work hard. Every day of our lives.

You see, it doesn't take much to let a beautiful dream go sour. All it takes is a few bad people getting busy, and a few good people getting lazy. At the end of the war I saw an America that was looked to as a beacon of hope and a bastion of liberty throughout the world, if not always by the governments, then certainly by the people. I'm talking about the guys who worked in the fields and the factories and the offices, who prayed in churches and synagogues, who dreamed of one day being able to raise their families in freedom, and who believed that America would be their champion. That's the way America looked to them then, and I thought that would last my lifetime.

Now I'm getting uneasy. I'm not saying it's gone, not by a long shot. But Americans who fought for freedom are being told today that freedom has its limits. There's a frenzy loose in Washington, where a man I know was hounded out of his job and robbed of his good name with nobody bothering to give a reason. "They don't need reasons," he told me. "Reason just slows them down. It's more like the fascism we fought than the principles we fought it with." The thugs in Washington are riding roughshod over the rights that looked so inalienable just a few short years ago, and if the real Americans don't speak up, those rights won't be there when we go to look for them.

I hear the people who run things may not be content to trample American constitutional rights. There's a certain popular government in the Middle East, a government of the people, by the people, and for the people, that is in very real danger of perishing from this earth. It could happen because there are shadowy, cold-faced men in the air-conditioned halls of Washington who think it suits their purposes, and don't believe there's anything that can stop them.

And it's starting to happen right now. There are forces at work in that certain country right now, buying the cooperation of newspapers, fermenting military unrest, coordinating street demonstrations -- hiring thugs to break windows and rough up storekeepers while carrying signs denouncing the government, then hiring more thugs to do the same while carrying signs praising the government.

When we start protecting America by denying freedom at home and imposing our will abroad, it may not matter anymore how many movies and automobiles we have, or even how much Jell-O. If we want to go on being the greatest country in the world, we need to think hard about what made us that in the first place.

Note: Jake Barnes will be on vacation for the next two weeks. In this space, enjoy columns by Art Buchwald next week, and Nicholas Carraway the following week.

(ENCRYPTED AND DECODED)
(4/17)
FROM: NICHOLAS CARRAWAY
TO: ALLEN DULLES

BARNES LEAK NOT FROM ME. BARNES MUST HAVE
HAD COLUMN IN BEFORE I HEARD FROM YOU.
I REMAIN A PATRIOT, WOULD NEVER REVEAL
CONFIDENTIAL INFORMATION. TELL ME WHAT I CAN
DO TO HELP TURN THIS SITUATION AROUND.

CARRAWAY

(ENCRYPTED AND DECODED)
(4/17)
FROM: LARRY DARRELL
TO: ALLEN DULLES

GOT AN OPERATIVE I NEED YOU TO INSTALL
IN EMBASSY IN TEHRAN. MAKE HIM CHARGÉ
D'AFFAIRES OR WHATEVER THE HELL YOU WANT TO
CALL HIM TO GIVE HIM STANDING. NAME: ALDEN
CARRAWAY. FILE BEING DELIVERED BY HAND.
CRUCIAL.

DARRELL

SPECIAL TO THE

New York Herald Tribune

APRIL 17, 1953

MOSSADEGH CHARGES DISTORTION ON IRAN

TEHERAN--PremierMohammed Mossadegh broadcast his thanks today to the Iranian people for their plebiscite vote dissolving the Majlis, then accused "some world statesmen" of misinterpreting and distorting events in Iran.

"Some foreigners endeavor to misinterpret and distort any step the Iranian nation takes to realize its aspirations because the Iranian people have forged a bond of unity and are resolved to cut off the hands that foreigners have extended into their country, which is the very thing of which a particular group is afraid."

(ENCRYPTED AND DECODED)
(4/18)
FROM: IRVING KRISTOL
TO: LARRY DARRELL

WHOSE HANDS IS HE TALKING ABOUT? STRONGLY
SUGGEST ABORTING MISSION.
KRISTOL

(ENCRYPTED AND DECODED)
(4/18)
FROM: LARRY DARRELL
TO: IRVING KRISTOL

DON'T WORRY. HE DOESN'T MEAN US. MOSSY
FIGURES IT'S THE BRITISH. HE WON'T KNOW WHAT
HIT HIM.

DARRELL

April 19

Dear Chris,

Trip was swell. Sat across the aisle from a young Danish wench who kept looking at me with contemplative gravity. Like she was sizing up a bull at auction. Displayed my return ticket prominently in my lap. As if to say catch me on the way back, honey, when I'm better prepared. Did I mention she was a nun?

Your Dr. Hamburger met me at the station. Eager sonofabitch, ain't he? Thought he was going to perform the surgery in the goddam cab. Positively effervescent after examination--I'm a textbook candidate-- of course, it's his fucking textbook--he's having the operating theater enlarged and inviting camera crews from Pathé News--and Louella Parsons and Dorothy Kilgallen will be on hand to broadcast the operation live over Mutual Radio. All contingent naturally on my okay.

Ah, there's the $64 question. Do I speak
now, or forever hold my piece? I feel like
you're the only person in the world who
might understand my dilemma, and then I
reflect that you went the other way and have
no idea what the fuck I'm talking about.
Don't mind me, Chris--we writing chaps have
words by the thousands--dozens, anyway--
to choose from, and I have but to make my
choice from two:

Yes or No?

Or there's Maybe ...

Love always,

Jake

Hotel de l'Odeon
Paris

April 19, 1953

Dear Ronnie,

I asked Jake if he had ever heard of Ruth
Brown, and he hadn't, but he knows this
little tiny shop where they have the latest
American records, and he went and bought
some of hers.

Then he went back to the shop a few hours
later and bought every record on your friend
Jerry's label.

I think Jake is really starting to miss the
USA. I'm not so sure I am. Except for one
person.

With much affection,

Nick

SPECIAL TO THE

New York Herald Tribune

APRIL 19, 1953

SHAH FLEES IRAN AFTER MOVE TO DISMISS MOSSADEGH FAILS

TEHERAN -- Shah Mohammed Reza Pahlevi and his Queen fled to Baghdad, Iraq, today after a coup attempt to oust Premier Mohammed Mossadegh had failed. Dr. Mossadegh appeared to be in complete control tonight, with the bulk of the Army apparently supporting him.

The attempt to remove the Premier was made at midnight. By dawn, Government forces had freed arrested officials, and had in their turn arrested Colonel Nasiri, commander of the palace guard, and scores of other persons, including military officers. The stroke and counterstroke were carried out without bloodshed.

The 72-year-old Premier clearly was master of the situation, at least for the time being, but the details of just what happened are confused.

(ENCRYPTED AND DECODED)
(4/19)
FROM: IRVING KRISTOL
TO: LARRY DARRELL

MISSION HAS FAILED. IMPERATIVE YOU GET OUT
OF IRAN AT ONCE.

KRISTOL

Hotel de l'Odeon

Paris

April 19, 1953

Dear Ronnie,

I received a cryptic note from Jake,
who has hied himself off to Denmark for
reasons unstated. So I'm alone with a
bottle of aquavit and my thoughts.

I'm glad you liked <u>Trimalchio in West Egg</u>.
I feel so damned distant from it now, and
yet in a way it feels like the only decent
thing I've ever done with my life.

After Jimmy Gatz died, when I sat down to
write about him, I didn't know I was going
to write a novel, or even what writing
a novel meant. Hell, I didn't even know
I was going to write. I just knew that
before I could get on with my life, I had
to figure out what had just happened.

The notes that became <u>Trimalchio</u> were the
beginnings of me trying to figure out
not just who Gatz was, but why he was so
damned important to me. The more I wrote,

the more the writing itself started to matter. I found that I didn't simply want to understand what was important; I wanted to find the words to express it.

As the days slipped into weeks, and the weeks into months--well, a few months-- the emphasis started to shift. I was still trying to figure out Gatz, but I found myself more and more loving the process of writing. I was going back over the stuff I'd written, not just to make sure I'd gotten it right, but to make sure I'd written it well ... and I didn't really even know what good writing was. I just knew that I was starting to hear words differently, and that suddenly I cared more than I could say about how words sounded, and how they looked when they started grouping together on a page.

I finished the writing, and I sent it to a publisher, and wonder of wonders, it came out as a book. It's like babies, or spinning gold from straw, I have no idea how it works. The book got a few good reviews, and a few bad ones, and was otherwise massively ignored by the incognoscenti. I suspect that the title didn't help. No one knew what the hell

"Trimalchio" meant. It's a literary allusion, which is the kiss of death-- the original Trimalchio was a character in Petronius's The Satyricon, a coarse parvenu who is respected by no one, and whose only entrée into polite society is his money. (Over here in France, observing Americans throwing their weight and money around, I wonder if our country may be the Gatsby, the Trimalchio, of the postwar era.)

So the book sank beneath the swells of public notice, and after Margery and I got engaged, it was understood that my little writing aberration was at an end. In years to come, my mother would refer to it as "that time when you had the flu."

Now ... it's probably too late. It's probably too late for a lot of things, and maybe I never had the equipment to start with. And I still don't know what good writing is. It's not too late for you, though. I remember when we hired you for Snicklepoo and the Baby Sitter. You were what ... nineteen? We were looking for someone who could relate to children, but could also project on television. To me, that meant someone who could sing a song. To our director, Jimmie Dodd, it meant,

"It doesn't matter how old they are. The only thing that sells on television is sex. What I'd really like is to find a girl who's just starting to develop, and let the audience tune in to see how much her titties have grown every week."

Oh, lord. I shouldn't have said that. But I'm trying not to edit myself with you anymore. Something's been growing in this correspondence, something every bit as mysterious and wonderful as the process Jimmie Dodd referred to, and I think we need to see each other one of these fine days to figure out just what it is. Your side of the Atlantic, or mine?

I listened to the singers you mentioned in your letter. Jake had a few of them, and I bought the rest from that little record store I told you about. I'd really never heard any of them, except Ella Fitzgerald. I liked all of them--especially Chris Connor. That smoky voice of hers reminds me of the youth I wish I'd had. It sounds like the way the Jazz Age should have been.

Love,

Nick

PS. Jake left his Trib column in my
custody while he's on his Denmark retreat.
I'm to split the duties with a young
fellow named Buchwald. I'm making him go
first. What the hell am I going to write
about?

SPECIAL TO THE

New York Herald Tribune

APRIL 19, 1953

SHAH TO GO ON TO PARIS

BAGHDAD -- Shah Mohammed Reza Pahlavi arrived here unexpectedly in his private plane after Iran's Premier Mossadegh had crushed an attempted military coup by officers of the Shah's Imperial Guard. With the Shah were his queen, Soraya, an aide and a pilot.

Neither had any luggage; piles of clothes belonging to the royal couple were strewn inside the twin-engined Beechcraft plane.

The Shah, 33, and his wife, 21, planned to travel from Baghdad to Paris. After high-level government consultations, they were escorted to the government's guest house.

The Shah's aide emphasized that he has not abdicated and did not intend to abdicate.

Meanwhile in Teheran, pro-Mossadegh mobs threw down from their pedestals statues of Shah Mohammed Reza. As crowds began battering the statue in Parliament Square, the Communists were driven off by police, but Nationalist, Paniranist, and Socialist bands were allowed to continue the destruction unmolested.

For two hours, men sawed at the ankles of the bronze statue, while others chanted songs written overnight on the flight of the Shah. Finally, a motorized crane was brought into action and the statue was toppled with a great clank amid loud cheers.

Similar anti-Shah sentiment was shown by the removal of virtually all his pictures from homes, restaurants, offices, and even Government Ministries.

(ENCRYPTED AND DECODED)
(4/20)
FROM: ALLEN DULLES
TO: LARRY DARRELL

OUR REPORTS SAY MOBS IN STREET HEAVILY PRO-
MOSSADEGH. YOU'VE BOTCHED IT.

DULLES

(ENCRYPTED AND DECODED)
(4/20)
FROM: LARRY DARRELL
TO: ALLEN DULLES

DOESN'T MATTER, AS LONG AS THEY'RE IN THE
STREETS. SITUATION JUST WHERE I WANT IT.

DARRELL

(ENCRYPTED AND DECODED)
(4/20)
FROM: ALLEN DULLES
TO: LARRY DARRELL

MISSION IS ABORTED. REPEAT, ABORTED. GET OUT
OF TEHERAN AT ONCE. TOO DANGEROUS. WE ARE NO
LONGER IN THE COUP BUSINESS.

DULLES

(ENCRYPTED AND DECODED)
(4/20)
FROM: LARRY DARRELL
TO: ALLEN DULLES

ARE YOU KIDDING? I'VE JUST BEGUN TO FIGHT!
CARRAWAY CARD READY TO PLAY. DO YOU REALIZE
WE HAVE A CHANCE TO OVERTHROW A REAL
GOVERNMENT? THIS IS BETTER THAN TANTRIC SEX!

DARRELL

(ENCRYPTED AND DECODED)
(4/21)
FROM: ALLEN DULLES
TO: LARRY DARRELL

WHERE ARE YOU? REPORT IN AT ONCE. I REPEAT--
WE ARE NO LONGER IN THE COUP BUSINESS. SHAH
PLANNING TO ANNOUNCE ABDICATION AFTER WE
DEBRIEF HIM. WE NEED TO HEAR FROM YOU RIGHT
AWAY.

DULLES

(ENCRYPTED AND DECODED)
(4/21)
FROM: P. RADCLIFFE JONES
TO: ALLEN DULLES

UNABLE TO LOCATE MR. DARRELL TO DELIVER YOUR
LAST CABLE. WHEREABOUTS UNKNOWN.

P. RADCLIFFE JONES, DEPUTY COUNSELOR OF

EMBASSY

Hotel de l'Odeon
Paris

April 22, 1953

Dear Jake,

Have fun in Copenhagen. What the hell are
you doing in Copenhagen?

I flipped a coin with Buchwald. He lost, so
he goes first on babysitting your column.
He tells me he plans to do an exposé of the
New York Yankees. He claims they have a
deal with the Devil, and he has the papers
to prove it. I intend to follow up with a
column on the scandal of escargot farming
in the Parisian sewers. Little girls on
leashes forced to sniff them out, fed
only on martinis. The little girls, not
the escargots. Or maybe both. I'm still
investigating.

Yours in journalistic solidarity and abject
terror,

Nick

PS. Tell me something. You're a man of the
world, or so I've heard--mostly from you,
as I recall. I probably couldn't have asked

you this in person, but I'm sitting here
in this ridiculous French bathtub with my
knees tucked up under my chin holding the
sorry remains of a bottle of aquavit, and
I'm thinking about something Margery said to
me more than once. She said I could never
make a woman happy because of the way I was
built. You know, the old tool of manhood
department. How about it, Jake? Is size
really the measure of a man?

Give my regards to Hans Christian Andersen.

Teheran, April 23

Alden--

   Can't meet you in person. I'm laying
low. I've arranged for you to meet
with Dr. Mossadegh. Your diplomatic
standing is all set. Tell Mossy that
as a representative of the American
people you're concerned about American
families who are being harassed.
Tell him that innocent children are
answering the family phone and being
subjected to unspeakable threats and
vile language. Tell him that you're
appealing to his sense of decency and
fair play to do something about it. Be
yourself, kid. You have that American
openness that he likes.

Larry

April 23, 1953

Dear Christine,

Get a load of the enclosed PS from Nick. Is
he trying to drive me CRAZY????

I've given the okay to Hamburger. The Stein
Ericksen of sex surgery set to schuss
tomorrow morning at 10. I'll be damned glad
when this thing is over. Worst case, I
guess, is no worse than it's been the last
30 years or so. Best case--what the hell is
the best case, anyway?

Did you know that the Bible has a special
section for people like me? It's Deuteronomy
23:1. He that is wounded in the stones, or
hath his privy member cut off, shall not
enter into the congregation of the Lord.

Well, that tells you something, doesn't it?
The way I look at it, and I say this with
the full piety of someone who's never left
the Church, technically speaking, it tells
me that the Kingdom of God, at least for a

man, is a woman's cunt. There's probably no equivalent for women, which is maybe why women tend to me more devout than men. They have no Kingdom of God on earth to distract them.

Here's a question for you, my love. Now that you're a woman, do you think about sex less often than you did when you were a man? I'm being serious. Nick's a man, so he's got to think about it most of the time. By Christ, he talks about that damned cock of his all the time, or at least whenever he's tight. Jesus, I never saw a man so bloody insecure! But his gangster novel wasn't written with his cock. I wonder what his next book would have been like, if he'd written it. Says he's writing again now. Maybe he's ready.

As Mehitabel says, toujours gai, kid, toujours gai. All's for the best in this best of all passable worlds.

Your old Bear,

Jake

Teheran, April 23

Larry--

   I'll do it. And I appreciate
the confidence you've shown in me.
Mossadegh is no fanatic, I'm sure he'll
listen. And I'll emphasize that America
has no intention of interfering in the
internal affairs of a friendly country.

   I won't let you down.

Alden

(ENCRYPTED AND DECODED)
(4/23)
FROM: IRVING KRISTOL
TO: KIM PHILBY

MI5 WILL NEED TO COORDINATE WITH US ON THIS,
SO BE PREPARED. AFTER IRAN, THE FRENCH
GOVERNMENT IS GOING DOWN, AND WE'RE GETTING
OUR DUCKS IN A ROW IN INDO-CHINA. YOU SHOULD
HAVE ALL CODE NAMES ON FILE. IF WE PLAN IT
RIGHT, THE REDS WILL NEVER KNOW WHAT HIT
THEM. THE COMMUNIST STATES WILL FALL LIKE
DOMINOES, ALL THE WAY TO CHINA.

KRISTOL

April 24

Dearest Brett,

I've just had the most remarkable day of
my life. I met for over an hour with Dr.
Mohammed Mossadegh, one on one. What an
amazing man!

Dr. Mossadegh was grave but gracious. I
explained to him that I was there not
only as an American diplomat but as a
humanitarian, and he greeted me in the name
of humanitarianism everywhere. He added,
however, that since I was an American
diplomat, he felt it incumbent upon himself
to express his displeasure at the American
government's stated position of recognizing
the Shah as the leader of his country, when
the Shah was now nothing more than a fleeing
criminal, the leader of a failed coup.
I told him that I didn't know anything about
that, but that America has always stood with
the poor and downtrodden of this earth.

Then I got to the heart of my mission, the
harassment of American citizens in Tehran.
They get threatening phone calls, often
delivered to innocent children in language
to which children should not be exposed.

They are harassed on the street when going about their business--even nannies pushing strollers. Their automobiles are vandalized --headlights smashed in, tires slashed, upholstery ripped out. I appealed to him as a man of decency to do something about this situation.

He didn't say anything at first. Just looked at me. There was sadness in his eyes, and something more that I couldn't identify. I just got the feeling he had seen more, and felt more, and thought about more in his lifetime than I can ever imagine.

He sat quietly for a few moments longer, and I almost thought he had forgotten I was there. And maybe he had. Suddenly he stood up without looking at me, walked to a telephone in the corner of the room, and dialed the chief of police.

His voice was heavy. "I cannot countenance what is happening to visitors to our country," he said. "Ours is a culture of courtesy. We must put an instant and complete stop to all rioting in the streets. Thank you."

Brett, Larry was right. He understood Mossadegh perfectly. The man is a responsible leader. I believe Iran is in good hands.

Love,
Alden

PS. Larry says he has another assignment for
me. I'm not sure what it is, but it's in
Indo-China. I can't tell you how it feels to
be finally involved in a meaningful way in
doing some good in the world.

PPS. For reasons of security, and for more
personal reasons, I will be dropping my
surname and from now on using my middle
name, which is Pyle.

Kempinksi Hotel
Berlin

April 25, 1953

Dearest Jake,

   Do I think less about sex? Oh, much
less! I don't know how you men ever get
anything done!

   You know, for as long as I can remember,
I've been interested in what makes someone
one sex or another, and it's not always as
easy as you'd think.

   Have you ever heard of the slipper
limpet? You've seen them, even if you
haven't heard the name---they're little
shellfish, and you see them in clusters
at docks, like mussels, one on top of the
other.

   They're always one on top of the other,
with the girls underneath. Mmm, I like
that. The girls are also always a lot
bigger, which is a lot more common in
nature than you'd think. (So is losing
your male equipment, for that matter--with
some spiders, after the male is through
servicing the female, it breaks off inside
her.) The pile goes from big mamas on
the bottom to little males on top. But
the little guys on top are persistent.
They don't call this species <u>Crepidula
fornicata</u> for nothing. They'll extend

their little wee-wees down four, five, six shells, as many as it takes, till they find a female. So you'd think the guys in the middle would be having the most fun- -the lowest male and the highest female. But it doesn't work that way. You see, the big mamas on the bottom weren't always big mamas. Once, they were little males ... and as they grew bigger, they also changed sex. So the ones in the middle ... they really are in the middle. Not boys still, not girls yet.

I guess all my life, I've felt like a crepidula, mostly without the fornicata. But like that gender-jumbled fellow in the middle, and like that poor drill sergeant at Fort Dix, it means a lot to me to be held properly, by someone who'll give me strength and nurturing, erotic tenderness, and more than anything else, the sureness that it's _me_ he's holding.

I never felt more completely like that than I did with you. And let me tell you this, you old bear, you're all man--and you always have been. You're no crepidula. And whether or not this operation succeeds (and it will--Dr. H is a genius!), you'll never have to send your wee-wee out probing around corners and under shells. Any woman who truly loves men will be coming to you, if you let them.

We'll have our time together, I know that. Maybe not a long time. I can see

where your destiny is heading, even though
you can't, yet. And I'm destined to be
Christine Jorgensen, with all the good and
bad that it will come to mean, for the
rest of my life. But I'll always love you.

Good luck, darling! Break a--well, I'm
not sure what. Anyway, I guess by now the
deed is done! I can't wait to see you. All
of you!

Love, Christine

(ENCRYPTED AND DECODED)
(4/25)
FROM: ALLEN DULLES
TO: IRVING KRISTOL

WHAT'S GOING ON IN IRAN? MOSSADEGH IS TAKING
THE WEAPONS OUT OF THE HANDS OF HIS OWN
FOLLOWERS.

DULLES

SPECIAL TO THE

New York Herald Tribune

APRIL 25, 1953

EXTREMIST RIOTERS IN TEHERAN FOUGHT BY POLICE AND ARMY

TEHERAN -- Policemen and soldiers, said to be acting under orders from Premier Mohammed Mossadegh, swung into action tonight against rioting Communist partisans and Nationalist extremists. The troops appeared to be in a frenzy as they smashed into the rioters with clubbed rifles and nightsticks, and hurled tear gas bombs.

According to sources inside the Mossadegh government, an unidentified representative of an American peace group had called on Premier Mossadegh earlier in the day "for the purpose of discussing recent developments in Iran." No further information was available about the meeting.

SPECIAL TO THE

New York Herald Tribune

APRIL 26, 1953

ARMY SEIZES HELM ROYALISTS IN IRAN OUST MOSSADEGH

Ex-Premier and Cabinet Flee Mobs

TEHERAN--In a swift and bloody coup, Iranians loyal to Shah Mohammed Reza Pahlavi today swept Premier Mohammed Mossadegh from power. Two hundred were estimated to have died in the fierce last-stand battle at Dr. Mossadegh's heavily fortified home.

The Army, which appeared solidly loyal to Dr. Mossadegh earlier in the week, turned on its top officers today. Dr. Mossadegh's Chief of Staff and other top officers fled long before the day was over.

The troops and the police that took part in the overthrow were led by huge mobs shouting for the return of the Shah.

4/26/53

FROM: JAKE BARNES
ROYAL HOSPITAL, COPENHAGEN

TO: MLLE CHRISTINE JORGENSEN
KEMPINSKI HOTEL,
BERLIN

ECCE HOMO

JAKE

(ENCRYPTED AND DECODED)
(4/26)
FROM: ALLEN DULLES
TO: ROBERT COHN

NO PLANS FOR COUP IN FRANCE. ELBA IS DEAD.
TELL NEPHEW TO BACK OFF. REPEAT, ELBA DEAD.
BACK OFF.

DULLES

(ENCRYPTED AND DECODED)
(4/26)
FROM: ROBERT COHN
TO: IRVING KRISTOL

HEY, WHAT'S WITH ALLIE? HE GETTING COLD
FEET?

ROBBIE

(ENCRYPTED AND DECODED)
(4/26)
FROM: IRVING KRISTOL
TO: ROBERT COHN

COHN, YOU IDIOT, THIS IS SERIOUS. THE COUP
IN IRAN VERY NEARLY BACKFIRED. WE CAN'T TAKE
ANY MORE CHANCES.

KRISTOL

(ENCRYPTED AND DECODED)
(4/26)
FROM: ROBERT COHN
TO: ALLEN DULLES

ALLIE--DON'T WORRY ABOUT A THING.

ROBBIE

Hotel George V

31 Avenue George V
Paris 8eme
France

April 26

Christine baby--

I love Paris! I luv luv luv wuv wuv wuv
Paris! "Daddy" says it's decadent and full
of Reds, and they all hate us over here.
But I've found some places where they think
Americans are just the cat's pajamas. Have
you ever been to a club called the Chez Miao
Miao? I bet you have, you devil! And guess
who took me there? None other than Maurice
Chevalier!

So did you hear the news? "Daddy" made a
citizen's arrest today! He's been acting all
strange and sulky and I thought maybe he
was mad because I've been spending so much
time with Maurice, but it turns out he was
hatching this really ballsy whopper of a
supprise!

So you know that guy Kerraway who was at
your table the other night at that stupid
jazz club? You may not know it, but he

was a witness in front of Sen. McCarthy's committy. Well, it turns out he really _is_ a Red! It turns out he wrote a book a long time ago, called "Something-or-other with Egg," that the Commies have put in every library we looked at in every American embassy in Europe.

So--today "Daddy" marched right up to this cafay where Kerraway was sitting with his pal the Commie French writer Albert Camoo, and he arrested him!!!! Talk about gonads, "Daddy" may be a little guy, but he's got balls the size of coco nuts!!!!!!

Well it caused a ruckus, I can tell you. There must have been about fifty reporters and photografers, and they were all yelling stuff and popping flashbulbs and carrying on, the jerks! "Daddy" called over a frog policeman and demanded that he take these guys to jail, but the stupid cop didn't even speak English! But finally "Daddy" must have got through to him, because suddenly we were all headed down to the police station. That was when the gooey stuff started to hit the fan, if you know what I mean. Those froggy policemen, they call them John-darns, it turns out they're all Commies (no bull). They were shouting at "Daddy" (in French! arrigant sonsabitches!) and carrying on, and he told them he was going to call the

Marines to come in and declare Marshall Law which he can do. And I told them I was going to call Maurice Chevalier, which I can do, but "Daddy" gave me such a look!

And then they called the American Embassy who sent down someone called the Charge Guy of Fairies, who got Sen. McCarthy (!) on the phone in Washington, and finally they let Kerraway go under his own something or other, but all his books are being consecrated from the libraries and he has a suppena!

Anyway I have to run. Maurice is picking me up later to take me to the Follies Bergeres while "Daddy" is at meeting at the embassy. I'm running out of money so I "lifted" some from "Daddy's" wallet, don't tell!

Love and kisses,

Davey

(ENCRYPTED AND DECODED)
(4/27)
FROM: ALLEN DULLES
TO: ROBERT COHN

WHAT'S YOUR NEPHEW DOING? HAS HE GONE CRAZY?

DULLES

(ENCRYPTED AND DECODED)
(4/27)
FROM: ALLEN DULLES
TO: NICHOLAS CARRAWAY

WHAT ARE YOU GUYS UP TO? A CITIZEN'S ARREST?
WERE YOU IN ON THIS? YOU'RE SUPPOSED TO
CLEAR ALL PLANS WITH ME BEFORE YOU PUT
THEM INTO ACTION. THE FRENCH ARE GOING
NUTS! AND HOW THE HELL IS COHN PLANNING TO
DECLARE MARTIAL LAW IN FRANCE? STAND BY FOR
INSTRUCTIONS. FROM HERE ON, CRUCIAL TO DO
EXACTLY AS I SAY.

DULLES

(ENCRYPTED AND DECODED)
(4/27)
FROM: ALLEN DULLES
TO: ROY COHN

DOES THIS HAVE ANYTHING TO DO WITH ELBA?
OPERATION CANCELED--DIDN'T YOU GET MEMO?
YOU'RE EITHER INSUBORDINATE OR INSANE! WE
NEVER HEARD OF YOU. LET ME KNOW IF YOU NEED
ANYTHING.

DULLES

(ENCRYPTED AND DECODED)
(4/27)
FROM: NICHOLAS CARRAWAY
TO: ALLEN DULLES

OF COURSE I WASN'T IN ON IT. IT WAS THAT
IDIOT COHN. I HAVE NO HANDLE ON THE
SITUATION. BUT I CAN TELL YOU THE FRENCH
GOVERNMENT IS MAD AS HORNETS, AND THE
EMBASSY HERE IS WORKING LIKE HERCULES TO
CLEAN UP COHN'S MESS. I HAVE TO TELL YOU,
ALLEN, THINGS LOOK VERY DIFFERENT FROM HERE
THAN THEY DID BACK IN WASHINGTON. LOOKING
AT AMERICA AND AMERICANS FROM A PERSPECTIVE
OF NEARLY 4,000 MILES IS NOT UNLIKE THE
EXPERIENCE I HAD LOOKING AT LONG ISLAND
THROUGH THE BATTERED PRISM OF AN UNDERWOOD
TYPEWRITER. THERE'S GREAT AFFECTION, BUT
A CERTAIN CHILLING REALIZATION OF DARK
THINGS LURKING IN THE SHADOWS. I'M NOT
SURE, AS WE SIT IN OUR OAK-PANELED OFFICES
IN WASHINGTON, THAT WE'RE AS SENSITIVE TO
NUANCE AS WE OUGHT TO BE. I THINK IT MAY BE
TIME FOR A WHOLE NEW APPROACH. I SUGGEST WE
POSTPONE ANY FURTHER ACTION UNTIL YOU AND I
HAVE HAD A CHANCE TO TALK MORE. I CAN COME
BACK TO WASHINGTON, BUT NOT FOR A COUPLE OF
WEEKS. I HAVE A FEW OBLIGATIONS HERE.

CARRAWAY

4/27/53
FROM: MLLE CHRISTINE JORGENSEN
KEMPINSKI HOTEL
BERLIN

TO: JAKE BARNES
ROYAL HOSPITAL
COPENHAGEN

DAVEY WRITES COHN CITIZENS ARRESTED CARRAWAY
IN PARIS STOP DAVEY MOST IMPRESSED BY DADDY
STOP DONT THEY REALIZE NO OF COURSE NOT STOP
ARRIVING PARIS TONIGHT HOTEL DU LOUVRE. WHEN
ARE YOU BACK

LOVE CHRIS

4/28
FROM: ROBERT COHN
WASHINGTON, DC

TO: DAVID SCHINE
HOTEL GEORGE V
PARIS

DAVEY
JORGENSEN AT HOTEL DU LOUVRE STOP MONITOR
MAIL FROM BARNES STOP MAY BE SOURCE OF LEAK
STOP I WANT TO NAIL THAT BASTARD

ROBERT

4/28
FROM: ROY COHN
HOTEL GEORGE V
PARIS

TO: HON JOSEPH MCCARTHY
RUSSELL SENATE OFFICE BUILDING
WASHINGTON, DC

ARRIVE WASHINGTON 8 A.M. TOMORROW STOP WORK
HERE DONE STOP NEXT THE ARMY

COHN

Hotel de l'Odeon

Paris

April 29, 1953

Dear M. Camus:

I am delighted to accept your kind
invitation to read tomorrow evening at
Shakespeare and Company, if the invitation
still stands. I prefer to read selections
from Trimalchio rather than the work in
progress, which is not nearly ready for
the light of day. But I thank you for your
interest and encouragement.

Again, for myself and my country, my
profoundest apologies for your being caught
up in the insanity the other day at Deux
Magots. M. Cohn has been summoned back to
Washington, and I hope this embarrassing
episode will be soon forgotten.

Sincerely,

Nicholas Carraway

ROYAL HOSPITAL
Copenhagen, Denmark

April 29, 1953

Dear Chris,

Yes, wasn't that a fine mess? All hell
breaks loose, and me not in Paris to cover
the goddamn story. I always thought I had a
nose for news. Just goes to show, you add
a new appendage, the others go straight to
fuck all!

I figure that yahoo McCarthy was behind it.
Or maybe it was just the lackey trying to
impress his master, although I would never
have credited Cohn with the gonads for a
move like that on his own. A citizen's
arrest of Nick Carraway! I gather it damned
near caused a government crisis. You almost
have to give it to the little creep for
sheer unmitigated world-class cocked-up
showmanship.

Having said that, those sons of bitches make
me vomit. They're everything I hate about
America (is that your husky contralto in my
mind's ear saying, 'Jake, dear, doesn't that
mean they're trying to destroy everything
you love about America?') All right, and

from where I sit, they're doing a damn good
job of it. I hear even the Cincinnati Reds
are planning to change their name. Well, why
the fuck not? There haven't been any reds in
Cincinnati since the Palmer Raids.

And is there anyone left to stand up to that
mob? Winchell's gone farther to the right
than that petrified asshole Ed Sullivan.
Even old lefties like my so-called pal
Irving Kristol are saying, "Well, you know,
there really is a threat."

Yeah, there's a threat all right. Just
ask some of the guys who've been driven
out of the country. I got a letter from
Howard Koch, a writer friend who's on the
blacklist--the one they swear doesn't exist.
He wrote a movie called Casablanca about
ten years ago. No one much remembers it
today, but it was a hell of a flick. He's
in England now, and I've been telling him
he should just stay the hell away from the
whole craziness, but he's planning to go
back, in spite of the goddamn blacklist.

And then there's Nick. Nick's a decent guy,
and I'm glad as hell I've had this chance
to get to know him. I guess I can thank
McCarthy for that, so I take back all the
crap I said about the cocksucker. Well, like
the guy in Howard's movie says, everyone in
Casablanca has problems. Nick's may work
out.

I'd feel a lot better if I were back in
Paris. There's something going on--I'll find
out soon enough. Nick's coming to Copenhagen
to pick me up, and we're going to take a few
days for a leisurely drive back to Paris,
sampling the local vintages along the way.
I'm thinking a little detour might be
in order, if you're game. Let's you and
me rendezvous in Normandy. I'll have
Nick drop me off at a little inn I know
near St. Laurent-sur-Mer. I'll check the
exact address and cable you with driving
instructions. Meet me Thursday next. I was
there in '44 covering the invasion, and the
place still packs a hell of a goddamn wallop
for me.

Now I've got another beachhead to storm.

With love,

Jake (and my new pal, Little Jake)

(COPIED AND FORWARDED BY DIPLOMATIC POUCH
FROM ROY COHN TO ROBERT COHN, WASHINGTON
DC.)

May 2nd

Uncle Robert,

I'm back in Washington, and damned glad to be
here. How'd you like my little Paris surprise?

I thought someone should know this, and
frankly, I'm a little hesitant to tell
Dulles myself, because he's not going to
exactly like it. I think Barnes knows more
than he ought to about plans that he ought
not to know about. And I'm afraid it was
my former friend Davey who's responsible.
He's been going all dorky, sneaking around
and acting like he thinks he's some kind
of a spy. I saw Barnes's name on the phone
pad, and when I asked Davey he wouldn't say
what it was about, he just looked like a
cat who'd swallowed a cloak and dagger. As
I said, it's Davey who is responsible. I
can assure you I never told Davey anything
secret (no bull). It's not like we were in
bed together, ha ha.

Maybe you and Aunt Frances could have me
over for a home-cooked meal. I'm sick of
that frog food!

Your nephew, Roy

To: The Hon. Prescott Bush

5/2/53

Scottie--Dulles getting cold feet.
Not the man he was. We'll have to go
over him, not through him. If there's
a shakeup at the Company and I end
up in charge, so be it. If Ike looks
weak, a few swift jabs could rattle war
hero image, and set stage for a Bush
in White House next election. See how
chips fall. Meanwhile, need your son
to help with a little end around play.
Tell George to run all France cables to
and from Dulles past me first.

Robbie

From: Hon. Prescott Bush

To: Robert Cohn

5/2/53

Robbie--You get one shot. Then the
door closes. I've got plans for that
young man, and they don't include any
possibility of scandal.

Scottie

JAZZ NOTES FROM AROUND TOWN

by Francis Paudras
May 3, 1953

PARIS--Don't forget to "dig" the magnificent Sidney Bechet as he plays le jazz hot at the Café du Monde.

The always-appealing Blossom Dearie debuts her new ensemble, the Blue Stars, at Caveau de la Huchette.

The legendary American pianist Bud Powell, just returned to Paris from a series of concerts in Sweden and Denmark, played Monday evening at an emotion-charged evening at Shakespeare & Cie honoring the noted American novelist Nicholas Carraway for his heroic stand against McCarthy lackey Roy Cohn. M. Powell will be appearing nightly at Le Bar Negre.

Hotel de l'Odeon

Paris

May 3, 1953

Dear Jake, Father of Contemporary Journalism
and Contemporary of Fatherless Journalists,

We miss you here in the Center of the World.
Where are you, when all the good stuff's
going on?

You'll have heard of my fantastic dust-
up with the unspeakable Cohn. As your
friend Paudras would put it, "all Paris is
talking about l'affaire Carraway." I will
save the eyewitness report for when I see
you in a few days, but suffice it to say
it was a novel and not altogether pleasant
experience. Well, but what is a writer about
if not experience?

What made it particularly galling was the
timing. I was sitting in Deux Magots with
Camus, and he was just about to propose.
I was like the spinster virgin, fanning
myself, with "Yes! and Yes!" rolled up in
my tongue, waiting for him to make his
declaration. The Camus proposal was an
invitation for me to do a reading under his
auspices at Shakespeare & Co., but before he
could get it said (you know how he hems and

pauses) the little rodent Cohn appeared at my elbow, and declared me his prisoner!

The resulting scandale has made me the unlikely hero of the hour in Paris literary circles, and what was, I'm sure, to have been a modest little event with tea sandwiches and lemonade escalated into a Major Event, with a full bar and speeches and testimonials, and even music--what music!--from our friend Mr. Powell, who has just returned to town. Oh, and I read from Trimalchio, and everybody clapped like hell.

I could hardly believe some of the notables who turned out--Camus, of course, and Sartre and de Beauvoir, and Malraux. Picasso was there, and drew a caricature of me on a napkin that I will have to show you. The director Jean Renoir told me he wants to make Trimalchio into a movie with the title of Gatsby le Magnifique. He plans to cast Gerard Philippe in my role (an obvious choice, you'll say,) and Yves Montand as Gatsby, with Jean Gabin as Meyer Wolfsheim. Montand was with him, and could not have looked less impressed. But he has an undeniable magnetism, and I could imagine him in the role of a Gallic version of my tragic gangster.

I handled all of that pretty well, I think. It was later that I got rattled. A teenage French girl came up and told me that she

intends to sleep with every famous writer
in France before she turns eighteen, and
then to write a great novel. Her name was
Francoise something--Saggan, I think. She
looked me over with a frankness that made
me shrivel. She told me that her father
absolutely hated ugly people, which meant
that he took up with one beautiful empty-
headed mistress after another, but she liked
clever people. "Of course," she said, "they
can't be completely devoid of physical
charm. People who resign themselves to the
fact that they don't measure up physically
seem to me somehow indecent. What are we
looking for, if not to please?"

I excused myself and said I had to go to
the bathroom, which was not the place most
calculated to get me out of a mood of self-
doubt as to whether I would measure up to
Francoise's standards. I confess I hid out
in there. And when I came out, her attention
had shifted to Montand.

But I wasn't out of the woods. Next, I was
accosted by Simone de Beauvoir, who bore
down on me with wolfish eyes that made young
Francoise seem like a hamster. "So," she
purred, "the paradigm I have never been able
to resist ... that classic American species,
the self-made leftist writer." She seized me
in an intimate grip that robbed me of speech
and very nearly of manhood. But at that

crucial moment Sartre intervened, and saved what I shall call my bacon.

This time, I _ran_ for the bathroom.

What's wrong with me, Jake? Oak Park was never like this! Was I married too long? Am I just insecure and naïve, or am I really, as I fear, not equipped the way a man ought to be?

I know this is Paris, and I'm a single fellow, and I've gained a certain notoriety, and I should be taking advantage of it, not thinking about one girl all the time. A man has to sow some wild oats, doesn't he? And if I'm afraid of not being enough for a woman, better to find out on someone with whom it won't matter to me so much if I'm found wanting.

This must all seem so juvenile to you. Anyway, other than that I've been working. Writing and eating, tearing it up, and throwing it up. Oh, and in two weeks (!) Girodias is bringing out a new edition of Trimalchio, in his Traveler's Companion series. He's offered me a very handsome advance against royalties, which I may well need, as I don't know how long I'll be keeping my current source of income (which I'll have to tell you about, I suspect you've been wondering.) They call it an

advance because they promise it long in
advance of delivering the cheque. I expect
it will arrive shortly.

Very excited about our trip. Anything I can
bring you? Food, money, some of this surplus
of women?

Your Devoted Friend,

Nick

5/3/53
Mr. Cohn — The following was
intercepted from Barnes in
Copenhagen. Do I show it to D.?
        GHWB

DULLES - IN POSSESSION OF DOCUMENTATION OF
ELBA PLANS. WILL NOT HESITATE TO MAKE PUBLIC
IF OPERATION NOT TERMINATED IMMEDIATELY. YOU
KNOW I MEAN IT. PLEASE CONFIRM. BARNES

From: Robert Cohn
To: George H. W. Bush

5/3

Show D. nothing. I'll handle this.
  C

5/3

Mr. Dulles,
Here's a cable from Barnes. Await
instructions.

George H. W. Bush, Communications Center

(ENCRYPTED AND DECODED)
(5/3)
FROM: ALLEN DULLES
TO: IRVING KRISTOL

SEE ATTACHED FROM YOUR PAL BARNES. HAS HE
TURNED TRAITOR?

DULLES

(ENCRYPTED AND DECODED)
(5/3)
FROM: I. KRISTOL
TO: A. DULLES

WORSE. HE'S AN IDEALIST.

KRISTOL

(ENCRYPTED AND DECODED)
(5/3)
FROM: ALLEN DULLES
TO: IRVING KRISTOL

WILL BARNES KEEP HIS WORD?

DULLES

(ENCRYPTED AND DECODED)
(5/3)
FROM: I. KRISTOL
TO: A. DULLES

HE ALWAYS HAS.

K

5/3/53
FROM: ROBERT COHN
WASHINGTON, DC

TO: G. DAVID SCHINE
HOTEL GEORGE V
PARIS

DAVEY--GOOD WORK ON LETTER BARNES MUST BE
STOPPED STOP ARRIVING PARIS TOMORROW AM STOP
HIRE CAR WE'RE GOING TO ST LAURENT SUR MER

ROBBIE

May 3, 1953

Darling Nick,

Please listen to the enclosed recording.
Mr. Wexler took me into the studio this
week, and here is the result. A demo, they
call it--a demonstration record. Mr. Wexler
wanted to see what I sounded like with real
musicians--and what wonderful musicians they
were! The pianist is named Red Garland.
The bassist, Paul Chambers. The drummer,
the sweetest man in the world--next to you,
of course--is named Philly Joe Jones. And
so complex! If Mr. Wexler hadn't told me
to listen to the bass to get the beat, I
would have been lost completely. Then for
the instrumental break, he used a wonderful
young tenor saxophone player named David
Newman, who everyone--except me, of course--
calls Fathead!!!! Can you imagine??? I hope
you'll listen to my second chorus of "Lover
Come Back," after David's instrumental part.
After listening to his improvisation, I felt
like I understood the melody so much better.

"Lover Come Back." It could be our song,
couldn't it? And when you turn the record

over, you'll hear the song that I insisted
on doing, and you can guess why: "April in
Paris."

Much much love, my dearest man,

Ronnie

*(GIVEN BY HAND TO GEORGE H. W. BUSH FOR
ENCRYPTION AND TRANSMISSION)*
5/3/53
FROM: ALLEN DULLES
TO: GEN. RAOUL SALAN

CALLING OFF OPERATION ELBA. TOO RISKY AT
THIS TIME. REPEAT, ELBA IS OVER. AWAIT
INSTRUCTIONS.

DULLES

5/3/53
Mr. Cohn - Dulles is pulling the plug on Elba — see attached cable draft.
GHWB

5/3/53

George--Thanks for the heads up. Keep
letting me know everything that goes out on
this matter--BEFORE you send it. Substitute
this message:

Gen. Salan--Stand by for signal. Coded
message in Barnes Door Thursday Herald
Tribune. Dulles

(ENCRYPTED AND DECODED)
(5/3)
FROM: ROBERT COHN
TO: NICK CARRAWAY

DUCKS IN ROW. TOP SECRET INSTRUCTIONS FROM
DULLES: USE YOUR BARNES COLUMN TO RUN THIS
PIECE. IMPORTANT: NO CHANGES!

FRANCE REMAINS IN AN UPROAR, WITH CIVIL
UNREST SWEEPING THE COUNTRY, AND FROM WHERE
I SIT, THE FRENCH GOVERNMENT IS DOING
NOTHING. THE SITUATION CRIES OUT FOR A
FIRM HAND--CURFEWS, A STATE OF EMERGENCY.
THE RECENT UNREST IN ALGIERS HAS PRODUCED
LAWS IN FRANCE TO DEAL WITH THIS STATE OF
AFFAIRS. BUT ENFORCING THEM IS A MATTER OF
WILL, AND I HAVEN'T SEEN ANYTHING FROM THIS
COUNTRY'S CURRENT BUNCH OF COOKIE CUTTER
POLITICOS THAT SHOWS ANY BACKBONE.

IT'S A SURE SIGN OF A DEGENERATE CULTURE.
LAW AND ORDER HAVE GONE INTO THE TOILET.
IF I WERE A PARISIAN SHOPKEEPER, I'D BE
BOARDING UP MY STOREFRONT RIGHT AROUND NOW.
THE STREETS ARE GOING TO BE FULL OF PEOPLE
WHO ARE NO RESPECTERS OF PROPERTY RIGHTS,
AND MORE WHO ARE SIMPLY FED UP WITH A
GOVERNMENT OF SPINELESS CLOWNS.

THE REAL DANGER, OF COURSE, IS THAT THE
COMMUNISTS WILL TAKE ADVANTAGE OF THIS
SITUATION TO SEIZE POWER IN A CITY THAT'S
ALREADY FAR TOO COMMIE-FRIENDLY, AND THEN

GOODBYE TO A ONCE-PROUD FREEDOM-LOVING
COUNTRY. YOUR CORRESPONDENT HAS HAD PLENTY
OF EXPERIENCE WITH THESE COMMIES. DUE TO
A MISUNDERSTANDING INVOLVING THE INEPT
GOVERNMENT AND KEYSTONE GENDARMERIE, AND
SOME NONSENSE ABOUT A BIT OF LITERARY
JUVENILIA THAT I'D LONG SINCE FORGOTTEN, I
BECAME THE OVERNIGHT DARLING OF THE PINKO
SET. WELL, I'M HERE TO TELL YOU, THESE ARE
THE SORT OF PSEUDO-INTELLECTUALS WHO ARE AS
LIKELY AS NOT TO LATCH ONTO JERRY LEWIS AS
THEIR NEXT CULTURAL DARLING.

THE FRENCH GOVERNMENT, IF IT SURVIVES, WILL
HAVE A LOT TO ANSWER FOR. BUT THEN, FRENCH
GOVERNMENTS COME AND GO THESE DAYS LIKE THE
TOURISTS WHO VISIT THE EIFFEL TOWER. AND IF
THIS SITUATION CONTINUES, THERE WON'T BE A
LOT OF THOSE.

AS FOR ME, I'M READY FOR A VACATION FAR AWAY
FROM HERE. BACK IN AMERICA. MAYBE OUT WEST,
WHERE THE ASPENS WILL ALREADY BE TURNING.
THEY TURN IN CLUSTERS, BECAUSE THEIR ROOTS
CONNECT THEM. I NEED TO GET BACK TO WORK--
AND LIFE.

REMEMBER, CARRAWAY, DULLES EMPHASIZES NO
CHANGES!

ROBERT COHN

Hotel de l'Odeon

Paris

May 3

Dearest Ronnie,

I've just gotten the damnedest message from
a man I respect very much, a top man in the
Administration, with whom I've been involved
in the service of our country. He wants me
to use my guest turn in Jake's Trib column
to plant a piece of muckraking garbage I'm
to present as my own words. His orders are
to run it exactly as he sent it to me. It's
incendiary, it's insulting, and some of it's
incomprehensible--aspens turning in clusters
because their roots connect them??? What the
devil does that mean??? I have a terrible
feeling it's a coded message.

Dammit, Ronnie, I don't know what to do.
Loyalties! My first loyalty is to my country
and my government. But what about my loyalty
to Jake? If I betray his trust by putting
this poison into the paper, he'll never
speak to me again. It will make for a very
uncomfortable drive down from Copenhagen,
if he even still wants me to meet him after
this.

And Ronnie, what about you? How will you
feel about a man who could do this? I'll
have betrayed you too. But the inescapable
fact is: I can't betray my country.

I'm going out for a walk. And then I guess
I'll take this column over to the Trib,
where I'll deposit this letter to you in
their overnight pouch to New York. Instant
communication. One of the perquisites of
newspaper life.

Love,

Nick

17 rue du Dragon
Paris, France

May 4, 1953

M. Barnes,

I received a message from M. Bud Powell, and
met him as instructed at Le Bar Negre. He
handed me a packet of documents from you,
which he had smuggled into Paris hidden
inside his piano.

I made the mistake of giving him the
payment you had promised while I was still
inspecting the contents of the packet. When
I looked up he had disappeared.

I found M. Bud in a disreputable boite,
which indulges the unfortunate and illegal
French passion for absinthe. The green
poison had already worked its mischief, and
to my mortification he initially confused
me with M. Hugues Panassié, the noted jazz
critic and moldy fig, enemy of all that is
innovative.

I managed to break through his phantasm, and
you can imagine my joy when not only did he
recognize me, but he importuned me to stay
and listen to a new composition.

Of course, I had no choice. M. Barnes, you
of all men must understand. And you can

but imagine what it was like, sitting in
a corner of this filthy dive, surrounded
by prostitutes, pochards on the verge of
delirium tremens, incautious tourists and
predatory loubards, and three mangy cats,
listening to a new work of unparalleled
genius. M. Bud began with a simple, haunting
melody that resolved itself into a minor
7th chord, at once jarring and soothing, and
moved into a string of contrapuntally playful
arpeggios, beginning with the blues and
extending into the territory of fugue ...

But I digress. I was able to convince M. Bud
to come home with me, where I gave him a
cup of hot tea and put him to bed. I left,
locking the door behind me to keep him safe.
Then I went to find M. Carraway.

At the Herald-Tribune I was informed that he
had already dropped off his column. I tried
his hotel. The concierge told me that he had
returned to the Herald-Tribune. I understood
that the errand was growing urgent, so I
stopped for no more than a moment to look in
on M. Bud before making a line of bees for
the newspaper office.

I found M. Carraway in the composing room,
engaged in a heated argument with the
compositeur. I approached him with the
packet you had entrusted to me.

"M. Carraway," I said breathlessly, "I bring you a packet of information from M. Barnes himself! He instructed me to inform you that you should read it before writing your column."

"Thank you," he replied, "but I have just completed my column."

"Too late!" interjected M. le compositeur. "The earlier version you submitted has been set in type!"

M. Carraway turned on the man, and there was steel in his voice.

"Listen to me," he snapped. "You will tear out this column, and replace it with the one I give you now! The earlier version was a mistake, and its publication would dishonor Mr. Barnes. Nothing must go into this newspaper that will do discredit to Jake Barnes. Do you understand me?"

M. Barnes, you should have seen him! His resolve was like a furnace, and the poor man melted before him. Then M. Carraway turned to me, and these were his words:

"Tell Jake thanks," he said, "but I'm not going to look at the documents, whatever they are. I'll do this my way."

I picked up the packet and brought it home
with me, where it rests on my bedside table,
as M. Bud sits at the upright piano in the
corner, putting the finishing touches on his
new composition, "Hallucination."

Sincerely,

Francis Paudras

(ENCRYPTED AND DECODED)
(5/4/53)
FROM: NICHOLAS CARRAWAY
TO: ALLEN DULLES

I COULDN'T USE THE COLUMN YOU SENT ME. I'M
SORRY. BUT I JUST DON'T BELIEVE ANYMORE. I'M
THROUGH WITH ALL THAT. I'LL ALWAYS CONSIDER
YOU A FRIEND. BUT THIS IS A CLOSED BOOK IN
MY LIFE. THIS WILL BE MY LAST COMMUNICATION
TO YOU THROUGH CHANNELS.

NICK

Atlantic Hotel
Hamburg, Germany

May 4, 1953

Jake, you dear old bear,

You must be proud of your friend this morning. The way he socked it to McCarthy, and "the danger to the American soul, if our government continues its present course of sacrificing our humanity and the core of our democracy at the altar of cold war expediency." Wow!

I was interested to note, though, that he didn't use any of the documents I'd liberated courtesy of Clyde Tolson, and delivered to you. Did you decide not to give them to him?

For the first time since my operation, I've been experiencing phantom limb syndrome. And I don't mean a pain or an itch, either. Well, I suppose you could call it a sort of an itch.

I don't like it much. I wanted to get rid of that thing. I don't want it suddenly getting all hard and throbbing on me, and it not even there. What makes it bearable is knowing where it is now. And wondering if what I'm feeling at those moments is what you're feeling. Phantom limb syndrome or sympathetic desire? Either way, I want

to put it to rest. And something tells
me that in order for that to be buried
once and for all, <u>it</u> has to be buried
inside me.

   By the pricking of my thumbs,
   Something wicked this way comes.

   And the sooner the better.
   Oh, Jake, we're going to have such a
damn fine time together!

Love,

Christine

From the desk of:
Allen Dulles

By Messenger
5/5/1953

To: George H. W. Bush

I want to know two things. First, this cable
from Carraway, what the hell is he talking
about? I didn't send him a column. Who did?
Second, who have you been conspiring with?
You've got a future in this organization,
Bush, but you've been playing a dangerous
game. I'll tell you something--your father
can't help you. Prescott Bush is never
going to be president. But remember this--
his son could be, and his son's sons, if
you're willing to learn where the true power
lies, and who to listen to, and how to take
orders.

And remember this. If someone can't help
you, it's time to dump him, even if he is
your father.

Come straight to my office on receipt of
this. Immediately. And talk to no one.
Especially no one named Robert Cohn.

Dulles

14½ MacDougal Street
New York

May 5, 1953

My dearest Nick,

I sat down to write you a letter in which
I was going to tell you that whatever you
decided, it would be all right with me. I
know that you've devoted so much of your
life to an ideal of America. I know, because
I grew up the same way. I didn't serve in
a war, of course, but as a little girl I
felt like I was part of it, saving my little
cans of bacon fat and balls of tinfoil, and
planting my little victory garden. I used
to salute every morning when I came out to
water my string beans and radishes. But that
was Winnetka, in what feels like another
lifetime.

New York can change you. It certainly
changed me. But I was writing you to tell
you that you didn't have to change for me to
love you. I know that first and foremost,
you're an honorable man, and whatever you
decided, it would be honest and principled.
First thing this morning I went out and
picked up the Paris Herald Tribune. When I
saw the column you'd written, I just melted.
I was actually crying into my espresso at
the Café Figaro. (I go there a lot; it's
just down the block from me, and the walls

are all covered in French newspapers, so it
makes me feel somehow closer to you.)

There's a spring warmth in the air that's
found its way even into the concrete canyons
of New York, but that doesn't explain the
way I felt. I was warm and tingly all over.
I had to take several deep breaths before I
could even go back to focusing my eyes on
what you'd written. You are my hero. If it
had been you sitting with me at that moment,
instead of just your words on a printed
page, I would have jumped right over the
table and smothered you with kisses.
Oh, Nick, I do want to smother you with
kisses. I want to hold you in my arms. You
must feel it too. Say you do.

But when will we ever see each other? I
loved what you said at the end of your
column, about finding what you had come to
think of as a realer America than you'd ever
known in the musical voice of Bud Powell and
the expatriate American voices of musicians
like Sidney Bechet and Blossom Dearie. But
does this mean ... you're never coming home?
I miss you so much, my darling, it makes me
ache.

Love,

Ronnie

Maurice Chevalier

5/5/1953
By messenger

General Salan:

The message in today's column has been
cleverly concealed, but it appears to be
embedded in the list of obscure names at
the end of the column--Bud Powell, Sidney
Bechet, Blossom Dearie. If these are
American entertainers, I am a resistance
fighter. None of them has ever appeared at
the Folies Bergère, I can assure you. And
that last name on the list is surely the
coded reference, to message 273: <u>We look
forward to the spring, when we take our
loved ones to see the cherry blossoms open
along the Potomac.</u>

Translation: Forget France. Devote all
your efforts to suppressing those towel-
headed colonials in Algiers. Be as brutal as
possible to the bastards.

Vive la Falange,

Maurice Chevalier

5/6/53

FROM: NICHOLAS CARRAWAY
HOTEL DE L'ODEON
PARIS

TO: JAKE BARNES
UNIVERSITY CLINIC
COPENHAGEN

ARRIVE COPENHAGEN TOMORROW STOP BE PACKED
AND READY TO ROLL STOP NICK

Jake Barnes
Copenhagen, Denmark
May 6, 1953

Dear Chris,

Nick did me proud. He found that one true sentence, and went on from there.

I did send him the documents. I wasn't going to. I used them as leverage on that bastard Dulles, and in return, I told him they'd go no farther than me. But I started getting a strange feeling in the old short hairs. There was a tap on my phone, and I'm pretty sure somebody was reading my mail. So I decided to let Nick decide what to do with the documents. And as you can see, he went his own way.

It felt like a valedictory, didn't it? Disillusionment can set in hard, once it sets in. I don't know if our boy is ever going back to America. Well, I know what that feels like, don't I?

Sympathetic desire, eh? It could be. I've been getting those same feelings too ... the old pneumatic pump is working the way it oughta. Pending the real test.

Nick is picking me up in the morning, and we'll be heading south. Get ready for the corrida!

Love and anticipation,

Jake

May 8, 1953

My dear Carraway,

A brilliant article. You succinctly captured
the existential failure of the nascent
American empire. I hope it will be the first
of many. I would like to see you writing a
regular column for Libération. Say the word
and I will approach the editor.

Camus

United States Information Agency
20 rue Lacepede, Paris 5e, FRANCE

May 10, 1953

Dear Ronnie,

I returned to Paris this afternoon to find
your wonderful letter and a parcel from you
at the hotel. A letter from you is always
occasion for excitement--but a parcel! I
tore it open with impatient fingers to find
your record (demo, is that what you call
it?) inside.

Of course I don't have a record player, but
there's one at the USIA library, and that
is where I have been ever since (note the
liberated stationary). I have been tucked
away in the audio booth for the last three
hours listening to you sing "Lover Come
Back" and "April in Paris" over and over
again, and I still can't believe it. My
God, Ronnie, where did it come from? You
always had a voice, but I swear, hearing you
do the show's theme song, "Snicklepoo and Me
and You," never prepared me for where you've
gone with it. There are emotions threaded

through your delivery that I don't think
I ever felt until I heard you sing these
songs. I feel almost criminal now, locking
you into that kiddie show for three years
when there was this *artist* waiting to burst
out! My God, Ronnie--my God!

Time and distance are measures I can't quite
put into perspective these days. I feel
I've been gone for years, not months. The
distance between us seems more like light
years than the few paltry thousand miles
that either of us could annihilate in a
matter of hours with an airplane ticket.
What's been happening to us, Ronnie? Is
there anything left in you of the pigtailed
young woman I hired in Chicago? Is there
anything left in me of the pompous stuffed
shirt who pushed that contract across the
desk at you?

I wonder this because I want desperately
to see you, Ronnie, and at the same time
nothing I've ever contemplated has scared me
more. I keep telling myself I don't really
know this girl--this woman--and as the song
goes, how can you lose what you've never
owned? But I feel as if I can lose, and lose
a lot, and it may be more painful than I'm
ready to risk.

There are many reasons for this fear--our
ages, of course, and habits, and tastes,

and experiences, and a jester's pouch of other reasons. But I'd be lying to myself and to you if I didn't admit that there is one issue that scares me more than all the others. It's a small thing, in a way, and yet it casts a shadow I may not be able to overcome. It seems to have been a problem in my marriage, although one I was never aware of until the end, and since, in which time Marjorie has not stinted in drawing it to my attention. It's a thing I could never address in a letter, and yet that may be the only way to do it, because I know I'll never be able to broach it in person.

So here's what I'm going to do. I've just returned to Paris after my drive down from Denmark with Jake. I dropped him off yesterday at a little inn along the Normandy coast--I'm pretty sure he had an assignation lined up, but he was being damned mysterious about it.

In fact, he still hasn't told me what his business in Copenhagen was, but I have the feeling he was getting hold of something important. There's a different quality to him, Ronnie, a kind of swagger I've never seen in Jake before, and I don't yet know what to make of it. But that's for another letter.

What I'm going to do, now, is to tear out a
few pages of my journal from the trip, and
include them here. I wrote these entries for
myself, so they address the subject with
a lack of self-consciousness that I could
never manage if I were telling the story
directly to you.

There are words in it I would never use in
front of a young lady, and I am mortified
to put them in front of you. But I feel
this is something too important to avoid.
If this offends you, I understand. I won't
expect to hear from you for a while; and
if, after some time, you feel like picking
up our correspondence again as if nothing
had happened, and keeping the distance and
relationship between us as it has been, a
sort of confessional exchange between a
middle-aged man and his young protégé, I
will willingly slip back into that harness.

So--read it, and if necessary, weep. The
reassurance Jake offers me here on this
matter of my agonizing uncertainty is
not the point. He calls it a matter of
perspective. His is one thing, Marjorie's
another. The one that will matter is yours.

With love,
Nick

From my diary —

<u>May 6 - On the train to Copenhagen</u>

On my way to Copenhagen to meet Jake. He still hasn't volunteered anything about the purpose of his trip, and unless he brings it up, I'll respect that. But he has been very urgent that I come up to meet him so we can drive back to Paris together. Once I learned that he'd liked my column, I didn't need much convincing.

Jake has arranged the hire of a car. I am to pick him up tomorrow at the University. We'll wend our way down through Germany and the Pays-Bas + maybe carve off a little taste of Belgium, partaking of the local wines + the fat of the land, talking about writing, and having a rare old time.

After the tumult of the past weeks, it will be both a pleasure and a relief to be away from Paris, adrift like Huck + Jim on a river of idleness, letting the current of conversation carry us where it will. I know I can learn a lot from Jake. Rediscovering myself as a writer, being taken up by the Paris literary world, has been the most exhilarating experience of my life. I feel invigorated + intoxicated. It's as if someone has reattached my male equipment after years of my not noticing the stuff was missing.

Speaking of which, one of the highlights of my evening at Shakespeare + Co came after the reading when de Beauvoir backed me against a bookcase + grasped me firmly by the crotch while looking me over like a woman choosing a cut of meat at the butcher's. I was at a loss for words, and might have lost more than that. Happily, Sartre came by and said something sharply to her in French, and she released me with a very Gallic shrug. I gave him an embarrassed nod of thanks, and he returned a sardonic smile.

Am I just enjoying the celebrity? Or is it the writing I crave? And can I still do it? By the time Keats was my age, he'd been dead for 30 yrs. But then, so have I.

May 7

Picked up the car. It's a pre-war Renault convertible, the color of egg yolk. Cloth top resists all efforts to put it up. We can only hope it doesn't rain. The thing runs, anyway, and the evil garage man who gave me the keys swore it has a full tank of gas — no way of telling, as the gauge is busted. Sitting outside the Royal Hospital waiting for Jake. Impatient to start the trip....!!!!

May 7 - night

Jake came down to the car — bounded, you might almost say — tossed his suitcase into the boot, clapped me on the back, + sang out "Come on, Nicko me boy, let's roll!"

We sped along through the Danish countryside, stopped for a late lunch at an inn where there was no English and little French spoken, but where we nevertheless managed to get a good meal of very fresh monkfish + a crisp white wine.

Clouds were gathering in the west as we left the inn. We wrestled with the soft top, + managed to rip it clean off its rusted moorings. We laughed hilariously, + left it propped up as a shrine on the side of the road. Jake was in exuberant spirits, which even the drenching rain didn't seem to dampen. Nor did the discovery of the garage man's treachery, when we ran out of gas. I was able to wave down a truck + get a lift to a gas station, but we lost a few hours + have wound up stopping here on the island of Funen for the night.

Found a wonderful inn with sloping thatched roofs + ivy on the walls + red + white flowers in neat beds + windowboxes. We were able to change into some dry clothes and tuck into an excellent dinner while management arranged our wet things by

the kitchen fireplace. Jake flirting broadly
with the innkeeper's wife as she served us,
which amused her but not the innkeeper.
I've not seen this randy side of Jake before.
He seems positively giddy. Maybe it's the
wine, or the Danish climate.

May 8 —
 Jake's asleep. I can't sleep. What a
day!
 Made our way by ferry to the mainland,
and tootled south, keeping to the coast +
crossing into Germany by lunchtime.
Jake entertained me with a rollicking
rendition of "Barnacle Bill the Sailor",
trilling the maiden's falsetto parts +
growling Bill's bass parts, + howling with
laughter. It was hard not to be infected
by his mood, and after we stopped at a
farmhouse + Jake disappeared inside +
emerged with a basket of bottles of local
wine, it became progressively easier
to join in the hilarity.
 After a few bottles I needed a piss.
We were on a straight stretch of road
without a farmhouse in sight.
 "I don't know if I can hold it," I said.
 "Why hold it?"
 "Well — but out here?"
 "Why the fuck not? Anybody coming,

we'll see 'em two kilometers away, if
that's what worries you." He flung
open the passenger door. "Tell you the
truth, I could use a leak myself."

I have always been a physically modest
man. In the years since I made the
transition to long pants I don't think I
have relieved myself outdoors more than
a handful of times — if I may be forgiven
the phrasing. I didn't play sports at Yale,
and managed to avoid entirely the naked,
towel-snapping camaraderie of the locker
room.

I had never even been to the men's room
with Jake. I preferred it that way — I tend
to use a stall if one is available — and
I always thought Jake preferred his
privacy as well.

So it startled the hell out of me when
Jake strode around the car + took up a
position next to me, + began unbuttoning
his pants.

"It's not going to do you any good in there,"
he chaffed me as I hesitated with my hands
suspended in front of my fly. "Come on,
Nick, don't be an old woman. It's just us
and the daisies!"

There are moments when doing something
embarrassing is less mortifying than prim
refusal. And so I found myself pissing onto

German soil, side by side with Jake. I couldn't resist a sidelong peek. To my surprise and relief his penis looked perfectly normal.

"For distance!" Jake challenged. I raised up + sent a vigorous stream raining on an anthill some four or five feet away. Jake's effort fell short.

"I haven't done this since I was a kid in the cornfields," I laughed.

Jake finished, and flicked. My effort continued a few moments longer, and I was aware of his eyes watching me with unembarrassed frankness.

"She's crazy," he said.

"Beg your pardon?"

"That wife of yours. Nothing wrong with the size of your cock. Maybe not quite as big as mine...." (here he drew his forward + twisted it between his thumb + forefinger with a pleased smile) "But hell, nothing to be ashamed of either. She's jerking your chain."

"Why would she say it, then?"

"She wants to put you out of business. That's it, pure and simple."

"I don't know. I can't tell."

"You're fine," he said, tucking himself back in. "It's the perspective, Nick. It's foreshortening, from the angle you look at it. It's a swell cock, Nick. Any woman

259

would be pleased as punch with it."

"You're sure?"

"Trust me," he said. "I've made a study of these things."

Jake Barnes
Saint-Laurent-sur-Mer

May 11

Dear Nick,

Into each life a little shit must fall. You will not believe what's gone on since you so blithely dropped me off at the shore a few days ago.

You'll have guessed that my rendezvous was with a lady. There are ramifications and implications and complications and sidebars that I may tell you about someday, but not now. When you're older. Suffice it to say I was looking forward with uncommon anticipation to getting laid, and so was the lady.

She never arrived. I waited at the Auberge Aubier until close to sunset, and then I liberated a bottle of whiskey from the bar and walked down to Omaha Beach. I had not been there in almost ten years. It was a warm evening and it was very fine outside and there were smells of cooking from the houses and the whiskey burned and it tasted good even if the lady wasn't there.

But the beach was not empty. It was alive with soldiers who jumped off landing craft with their rifles held over their heads and struggled through the surf and up onto sand that was churning with bombs and mortar shells. I could smell the explosives and hear their thunder and feel the impact of the shocks of the explosions and hear the shouts of the men and their screams. They were there, and they were real, and I was the ghost among them.

I sat on a dune and watched the troops storm the beach, and watched the assault, and felt the shells and the bombs exploding around them and all around me, and I drank the whiskey I had brought with me and I thought about the lady who had not arrived, and I wondered what had happened to her and why the bombs and the whiskey were not having any effect on me.

A man was walking toward me across the sand. He wore a hat, and a trench coat that was belted around the middle. He did not look very much different than he had looked thirty years ago, except that he had not worn the hat and the trench coat then. "Hello Robert," I said. "What brings you here?"

"Hello, Jake." Robert Cohn sat down on the dune beside me. "I've come to take you down."

"Well, have a drink."

Cohn took the bottle and drank, and I noticed that the assault had ended and the soldiers were gone and the beach was empty and quiet again.

"Look out there," he said. "That's Africa."

"Where?"

He pointed out to sea.

"No," I said, "that's New York. Africa's down there to the left, past Spain."

"Well, that's where you're going. Africa."

"I can't, Robert. I've got a date with a lady." I took the bottle back. "We'll go shooting in Africa some other time."

"There'll be shooting," he said, "but I'm not going with you. I'm sending you." He took his right hand out of the pocket of the trench coat and there was a gun in it. It was a MAS 50, a French Army pistol. "It's all arranged, Jake. I'm delivering you to a guy who recruits for the French Foreign Legion. You'll be in Algiers in a couple of days. Sorry. You're getting to be too big a problem."

The barrel of the gun made a short arc toward my head and everything went black.

I woke up in the dark and I found that my hands were tied behind my back and my ankles were bound too, and I was in a small confined space. I heard voices.

"Well look who's here." It was Cohn. "Who's your lady friend, Davey?"

"Hello Robert. This is Christine Jorgensen."

"The famous Christine Jorgensen."

"Where is he?" It was the voice of the famous Christine Jorgensen.

"Where is whom?"

"Who," Chris corrected.

There was a gag in my mouth, but the tape had slipped and I spat it out. "I'm in here," I said. I wasn't sure where in here was.

"Jake? You're in the boot?"

"Hard to say."

"Really, Mr. Cohn!" Chris sounded indignant. She sounded like my mother when somebody farted. Chris was a real lady.

I heard a sharp rapping over my head. "Open this trunk immediately!"

A key rasped in a lock, and the lid of
the trunk swung up. There was Chris. She
looked beautiful. Cohn stood behind her, and
behind him off to the left was Davey Schine,
looking pale and scared.

"These European cars aren't as roomy as the
American models," Cohn said. "It may get
a little tight in there." He gave Chris a
shove and she tumbled in on top of me into
the trunk. The lid slammed shut.

"Hello Jake."

Her mouth was very near mine, and I kissed
her. "Hello Chris."

The motor of the car started, and then it
stopped. We could hear Cohn's voice, and
then Schine's. They were talking, or they
were arguing, it was hard to tell.

"Is this the place you wrote me about?"
Chris asked.

"No, it's up the beach a bit. It is not very
big, but it's bigger than this."

"I was going to rescue you, but I'm not used
to the high heels yet."

"Don't worry about it," I said.
I see I'm writing a novel. I hadn't meant

to, but it started coming out that way. I just wrote that one true sentence, and then I went on from there. It's all your fault, Nick. It must be catching, this literary bug of yours. Take two slugs of gin and call me in the morning.

Anyway, here's what happened. All very dramatic and exciting, but not much to it really. If you don't count the gun.

And I don't count the gun. Not really. The Mas 50 is a Browning single-action with a slide-mounted safety. Cohn had some trouble with the safety, so I was able to conk him over the head with the tire iron when he opened the trunk. Chris had obligingly sawed my restraints with her nail file.

We got Cohn trussed up with the rope and gagged with Chris's nylons, and we tucked him into our old quarters. Schine knew where Cohn had set up the contact with the Foreign Legion guy, and he and Chris assured me Davey was on our side now. So I gave him the keys to Cohn's rental car and told him to deliver the package. I told him to tell the guy to make sure they keep the gag in. Tell him this Barnes guy is delusional and more than nine-tenths wacko, but he'll be a hell of a fighter once you get him to Algiers. Schine took the car and pointed it toward Marseilles. I took Mlle. Chris's arm, and

pointed her toward the inn. A curtain of
decency descends over what followed.

Your old pal unt lit'ry mentor and guide
through life,

Jake

Mars Say

May 14

Dear Roy,

Boy, your uncle is crazy! And so are you,
for that matter. All you Cohns are nutso!
Look, you better get me out of the army, or
I've got some things I could tell that a Few
People might be intersted in.

You'll be intersted to know that your Uncle
Robert has joined the French Foreign Legion.
I played a small part in his decision. Well,
maybe not so small. But he had it coming.
You know what he did to me?

So he asked me to hire a car and pick him up
at the Aura Lee Airport in Paris and he said
we were going to go on a road trip to this
place called St. Lawrence and stop Barnes.
So I picked him up. He was kind of spazzing
out, you know, and talking a mile a minnet.
So we drove a while, and I guess he thought
I had a map but I didn't have any map. I
mean why would I have a map?

So he got all in a conniption and then he
told me to stop at this little gas station
where they don't even sell gas they sell
essence if you can beleve it, and not cheap!
And he told me go in and get a map and I
told him you speaka da frog you getta da

map. So he gets all bitchy but he gets out
and he goes inside and he's in there a long
time and finally he comes out and he doesn't
have a map. He says they didn't have a map,
but he got instructions. Okay.

So off we go again and he keeps telling me
okay take a right here, and take a left
there, and on and on, and he falls asleep,
and next thing you know we're in this town
and there's a cathedral and your uncle is
saying so that's Rooawn the famous Cathedral
of Rooawn and Davey my lad it would be
good for you to see it because it's very
famous and Monay painted it. So we get
out and it turns out it's not Rooawn, its
fucking Orleans, where Joan of Ark and Louis
Armstrong come from, and which is in a
hundred percent the wrong direction.

So we had to turn around and head the other
way, and boy was your uncle pissed, but he
couldn't make it out to be my fault, even
tho he tried! And when I asked him about
stopping Barnes, I mean stopping him how, he
got all silent with me.

So anyway we lost a day, and we wound up
having to spend the night in this jerkwater
town on route, in this little dump where
they only had one room and it had a double
bed! So we had fun anyway, but in the
morning your uncle gets all weird on me, and
he tells me he wants to do this thing where

he ties me up, you know, like when we do that Gulliver thing? Well so anyways I say sure, and he ties me to the bed, and then he stuffs my underpants (the purple ones) in my mouth, and then he grabs his bag and says "So long, Davey," and out he goes!

Okay, I mean I like games. But after a couple of hours I'm starting to think maybe this ain't no game! So I start struggling and thumping the bed and trying to spit out the goddamn underpants, but I'm not getting anywhere and nobody seems to notice except once I heard someone yell up something in French that who knows what the fuck it meant but probly shut up. And then a while later the maid sticks her head in the room and sees me spreadeagled on the bed in the buff, and she just kinda shrugs and shuts the door!

So I'm lying there trying to figure out what the fuck to do, and I here a car pull up outside, and I here this voice say "Excuse me, parley-voo Anglay?" And I think holy crap I know that voice! And I make a mighty goddamn effort and I get the undies out of my mouth and I scream "Christine!"

And it _is_ Christine, you know, my friend I told you about that used to be a guy, I mean what are the fucking odds, right? So she gets me untied and I put my clothes on. And what do you think? It turns out she's on her way to St. Lawrence too, which is how she came to be on that little podunk road in that little podunk town and stopped at that little podunk joint to ask directions. And wait a minnet, you think that's weird? Guess who she was going to St. Lawrence to meet? Jake Barnes!

So I told her about your Uncle Robert and stopping Barnes, and man, she may not have been a girl long, but she can sure scream like one! So we piled into her car and took off in the direction they pointed us. We got to St. Lawrence about sunset, which is not a great time to be driving there because you are looking right into the goddamn sun the whole way. And we pull up to the beach and there's my car, the one I hired, and there's your doofus Uncle Robert.

And it turns out he's got Barnes in the trunk and next thing you know he's got Christine in there too! So he tells me to go get in the car, and boy, I'm shaking by now, because he's already left me tied up once today. So there's this pistol on the seat, one of those neat French Army jobs, and I take my gum and I wedge it under the safety.

And then Robert gets in and he picks up the gun and he starts up the car and he says okay, Davey, I'll take care of you later, which doesn't sound so good to me. And he hands me this piece of paper and he says

okay this is where we're going to Mars
Say and this is the guy from the French
Foreign Legion we're going to meet, and you
study these directions careful, you little
cocksucker, and if you get us lost again
I'll have your nuts. He could charm the
little birds out of the trees, your uncle.

And he tells me there's a sonofabitch I've
done some business with, Aly Khan, married
to Rita Hayworth. A real hardass, used to be
an officer in the Legion. Those Arab Muslims
know how to keep their people in line, not
like Mossydick and those bleeding heart
democracy cunts. We could learn from 'em.
Pick your nose, they cut off your finger.
Aly will make a call, make sure Barnes gets
personal attention.

So I ask him what about Christine, and
he kind of laughs and says the notorious
Christine Jorgensen, do you have any idea
what some of those whorehouses in Mars Say
would pay for her?

So I have the feeling that if we get started
I am so screwed, so I say wait a second,
I think I heard something back there, and
he says what, and I say I don't know but I
think you better check. So he curses and
stops the motor and gets out with his gun
and goes back to check, and I'm gonna slide
over as soon as he's out and drive off like

a bat outta hell, but shit he takes the
fucking keys!

And then I here something that sounds like
what the, and then umnph, and I get out and
there's your Uncle Robert stretched out on
the ground and Barnes climbing out of the
trunk with a goddamn tire iron in his hand
and blood in his eye. But Christine God
bless her tells him no no, Daveys with us,
which you can believe it I was!

So we tie Robert up and stuff him in the
trunk, and I tell Barnes about where Robert
was going to deliver him to this French
Foreign Legion guy, and Barnes kind of
smiles. And your uncle says no wait, Jake,
don't be crazy, and Barnes says what the
hell, Robert, what the hell.

Robert starts yelling, and Christine takes
off her nylons and shoves them in his mouth,
and Barnes slams down the lid, and hands
me the car keys. And he tells me they're
expecting Barnes, Davey, you take 'em
Barnes.

And I did. I drove like hell down all the
way to Mars Say and found the guy down at
the waterfront and the last time I saw your
uncle he was being loaded onto a freighter.
So listen Roy, I think you and me should
call it a day. That stuff's okay when you're

a kid fooling around, but I'm going to find
me a girl and settle down and do something
serious with my life. I'm thinking of going
into the movies. Anyway I'm sure as hell not
going into the Army, so you get that squared
away, okay, for old times sake? That way
all our little secrets can stay our little
secrets.

Your pal,

Davey

May 17

Lady B--

Well, I never thought I'd be writing you
about this, although I imagined doing it
with you often enough. Hell, I imagined
doing it often enough. But here's the scoop.
I'm all there now, and it works. It goes
up and down. I could change a tire with
it. Better than that, I can do what it's
designed for. Have done it. The old in and
out. Well, I am here to tell you, that's
exactly how it works. In. And out. And in.
And out. And in ...

Yeah, yeah, you know all about it. But
here's the catch, your ladyship. You don't.
You don't know a damn thing about it.
Nothing can be sole or whole that has not
been rent. Now I am the king of the cats.

And one more thing, milady. I'm glad it
wasn't you.

Formerly yours,

Jake

Mlle. Christine Jorgensen
Dover Inn
Dover, England

May 17, 1953

Dear Davey,

   Good luck with staying out of the
army. I hope Roy and the Senator can
fix it for you, although frankly, I
wouldn't count on either of those two
to find a giraffe in a broom closet.
   Meanwhile, I know you're wondering-
-what happened after you left for
Marseilles? How did it go? Well, it
went ... and went ... and went. And was
divine.
   Hard as I know it is for you to
believe, my adorable little hormonal
handful of horny youth, I didn't just
undergo this major surgery in order to
try out some new sex positions. Not
that I'm saying that would be a bad
thing. After all, it's basically why
Jake had his operation, and I'm so glad
that he did.
   No, there was much more to it
than that, and I know you're not the
slightest bit interested in any of the
rest of it. So ... it was lovely. Jake
was the right man for me in so many
ways. We talked, and we drank, and we

took our clothes off, which was not
quite the easiest thing for either of
us. We felt like prepubescent kids.
There was a lot of looking, and a lot
of touching, gingerly at first. And
when it happened, I felt somehow as
though I'd been made whole, for the
first time. As though for the first
time that thing actually fit me.

I don't know that there'll be a lot
of sex in my new life. There'll be a
lot who won't want me, and a lot who
will want me for the wrong reasons,
freak show reasons. And I don't have
the most active libido in the world. So
these past few days may have to make up
for a lot. And believe me, they will,
they will.

I woke up very early this morning.
Jake was still lying asleep, on top of
the covers. I looked down at him. That
thing between his legs. Once it had
been the symbol of everything I hated
about myself, everything that made me
wrong, a freak, a stranger in my own
body. Then for a glorious moment in
time, it had been hard and straight and
a connection of love between me and,
quite probably, the only person who
will ever understand me. Now it was
nestled peacefully where it belonged,
and I said an easy goodbye to it, with
a tiny kiss, and a fond goodbye to its

new owner. I tiptoed out early this morning, and caught the boat train. I left a note on Jake's pillow. It said: I'll always love you, you old bear, and good luck in America. That's where you're going, whether you know it yet or not.

Your pal and partner in crime,
Christine

14½ MacDougal Street
New York

May 19, 1953

Dearest Nick,

I wouldn't have believed it was possible
for a man to be so open and honest and
vulnerable. Certainly not in Winnetka, and
you know something? Not in New York, either.
Men are the same all over. Except for one.
One wonderful man, and it's too wonderful to
be true that he cares about me.

I'm not a jazz singer. Not yet. But Jerry
Wexler thinks I can be, with about three
years of very very hard work, and practice,
and study, and a lot of singing. He says I
can find the practice and study in New York,
but it's a hard town to do an apprenticeship
in. He's given me a letter of introduction
to a great singer and teacher named Blossom
Dearie, in ... Paris!

I can move to Paris and study and sing.
And I'm sure I can find a cheap place to
live. I met this friend of Jackie's who's
working in the theater business, who just
came back from studying at the Sorbonne,
and she's told me all about the cafés and
museums and sitting by the Seine, eating her

lunch of bread and cheese and ... if she
felt especially rich some days ... a tomato.
It all sounds wonderful. I can get a small
place and ... unless ... Oh, Nick, write me
back and tell me if you want me to come!

Love,
Ronnie

Rue Catinat, Saigon

May 19, 1953

Dear Dad,

Long time no write.

I'd like to introduce myself. I feel like
I've been through about a dozen lifetimes
since we last saw each other. And now I see
this column you wrote in the Paris Trib, and
I can't believe you're the same man I fought
with so much before I left home. We'll have
a lot to talk about when next we meet.

I'm in Saigon. I can't tell you much more
than that, except to say I'm attached to
the Embassy in an advisory capacity. So,
in a way I'm sort of working for your old
firm, right? And you're a writer, and living
in Paris. I guess we've kind of come full
circle, haven't we?

I've become good friends with Fowler. You
met him in Paris. He's a good guy, a bit
cynical and unengaged, but that's the
problem with all these old European types.
The more I travel and the more I read, the
more I've come to realize that in this world
you've got to choose sides.

I've been reading a lot of York Harding
lately. (He's actually my friend Larry

Darrell, writing under a pseudonym.) Do you
know his books? The Role of the West, really
interesting, really profound. And some
articles in Encounter.

Anyway, I think I can do some good here,
in a quiet way. The French have made a
thorough botch of things, but Vietnam can't
be allowed to fall to the Communists either.
I've got an idea that a Third Force can
be created that will act as an indigenous
insurgency against both of them, and pave
the way for the establishment of a truly
free democracy in Southeast Asia.

I've met a girl. That's complicated too.
And it involves Fowler. But that's all for
another time, when I see you.

Affectionately,

Alden

May 21, 1953

Dear Jake,

It's been a couple of years since I wrote
asking you to join my team for this
television adventure I've embarked on, See
It Now. Your reaction at the time, as I
recall, was, "I wish goddamned television
had never been invented." Words, as you
know, I have uttered myself. In fact I
suspected at the time you were quoting me,
in a not-so-subtle dig at this reporter's
selling of himself on an altar of tubes,
wires, and breakfast cereals.

You may not have noticed, over there in
Europe, but the damned medium seems to be
here to stay, and I believe it has the
potential for significant importance as
well as virtually unlimited triviality. I'm
looking to shore up my team here at See It
Now, and I'd like to have you on board, old
friend. There is big game to be hunted, and
this is an adventure you will not want to
miss.

You've been in Europe long enough, my
friend. My guess is, we're fed up with

pretty much the same things, and the same
people. Let's take them on together. The
danger is in America. And danger was always
something you had a nose for.

Warm Regards,

Ed

Jacqueline Susann
100 Central Park West
New York, NY

June 15, 1953

Dear Ronnie,

Well, sweetie, Paris is three thousand miles
from Broadway, but as long as you're happy.
If you see Coco Chanel, give her my best,
and ask her if she still likes being pinched
on the ... well, maybe not.

Just make sure that guy you're with does you
right. You know how men are--they won't buy
the cow when they can get milk through the
fence.

And check out my new address--and the new
stationery. I met a fella who fit all my
requirements. He's older (think yuck), but
I've talked him into separate bedrooms and
ya know, you don't have to buy the bull to
get ... well, you get the idea.

He's Jewish ... and is he ever Broadway.
He's a super press agent, and he tells me if
I stop popping those dolls and start writing
about them, he can guarantee me a best
seller.

Drop me a line one of these, days, kiddo.

Your old pal,

Jackie

Mrs. Nicholas Carraway
Paris, France

July 21, 1953

Dear Jackie,

Wondering what happened to me, girl? I want to thank you for the friendship you extended to a dumb kid from the Midwest, and for all your sisterly advice, although I'm afraid I didn't end up taking much of it. Forgive me? But it all worked out for the best.

Nick and I were married last Friday. Blossom Dearie, the American singer, was my maid of honor. Albert Camus, the French writer, was Nick's best man. He had wanted his friend Jake, but Jake couldn't leave his work--he's in the middle of a big project with Edward R. Murrow, a television documentary about Senator McCarthy. Not only that, he's become close friends with my old mentor, Jerry Wexler, and he's going to start producing some jazz artists for Atlantic Records. And as he wrote to Nick, "Right now, the only thing that would get me out of New York with a crowbar would be a trip to New Orleans or Kansas City or Memphis."

I'm studying with Miss Dearie, and singing nights in a little cabaret. I even got to be a backup singer on a record Miss Dearie made--"Lullabye of Birdland" in French!

Nick works on his novel every day. I'm more
or less supporting us until he gets his
advance from M. Girodias, although M. Renoir
has paid him to option the movie rights for
Gatsby le Magnifique. But I don't mind. It's
so exciting to see how he glows with an
inner fire after a day of writing.

And ... married life is wonderful. We've
actually been ... you know, without benefit
of clergy, since I arrived in Paris. You can
do that over here.

The only thing ... just between us girls ...
I mean, I don't have much to compare with,
except whatsisname ... but down there, he's-
-you know, a little bit ... smallish? But
that doesn't really matter, does it?

Love,
Ronnie

ACKNOWLEDGMENTS

If this section were to be done right, it would run to book length all by itself. There are so many people, so many sources, that help push a project like this along.

One of the first to nudge this book from the talking stage to the doing something about it stage was Jim Idema, a great newspaperman and a great friend. I mentioned the idea to him over lunch one day, and he wouldn't let it alone. "When are you going to write that story about Nick Carraway and Jake Barnes?" Jim lived long enough to read the first draft, and he loved it.

Agent and former publisher Don Lamm liked what he saw. He provided early encouragement, and great help and advice every step of the way.

Sue Manocha, Claudia Jessup, India and Alex Richards, Ted Brooks, and Jenny Hickey copy edited and proofread the manuscript. Peter Jones gave advice and guidance.

We had the incredible good fortune to find the exact right editor in Lilly Golden, who understood and supported everything we were trying to do.

Thanks to the art department at Skyhorse for coming up with a great design and listening to our suggestions.

And a special thanks to two guys named Scott and Ernest, even though they don't exist.